THE FORTUNES OF TEXAS

*Follow the lives and loves of a complex family
with a rich history and deep ties
in the Lone Star State*

DIGGING FOR SECRETS

A ruse brings six estranged Fortunes to
Chatelaine, Texas, to supposedly have their most
secret wishes granted. They're thrilled—until
they discover someone is seeking vengeance for
a long-ago wrong...and turning their lives upside
down!

Fortune in Name Only

Asa Fortune can't believe it when his dream
ranch is slipping out of his grasp...just because
the ladies' man hasn't yet walked down the aisle!
So when his agreeable best friend, Lily Perry,
agrees to a six-month marriage, he can't believe
his good luck. And he really can't believe when
Lily ignites a fire in him he desperately needs to
extinguish. After all, this union is only temporary.
Or is it?

Dear Reader,

I'm so excited to be an official part of the Fortune family! If you're new here, you're in for the best of the best. The best stories that grab you up and take you to a place you want to be. Stories that engage all the emotions and leave you feeling not just satisfied, but smiling. And the best news there is...there are always more Fortune stories to devour! You don't ever have to leave this newsworthy family!

If you've been with the Fortunes for a while, you already know all of that. And welcome home.

And this particular Fortune story...I got all the feels writing it that I always get when I'm lost in reading romance novels. Lily is a true heroine. Someone I admire. Someone I want to be. She didn't have a perfect, or even pretty, life. And yet, every day, she looks for the good. And Asa—well, he's a work in progress. Aren't we all? Mostly what I love about this story is the possibility that awaits when you have the courage to take a risk. To go off course for a chance to find happiness. I learn from all of my books. My characters teach me as they evolve inside me. And this one...I've taken a big risk this week, one I haven't taken before, but wanted to, because Lily showed me the way.

I hope her special approach to life blesses you, too.

Tara Taylor Quinn

FORTUNE IN NAME ONLY

Tara Taylor Quinn

Special thanks and acknowledgment are given to
Tara Taylor Quinn for her contribution to
The Fortunes of Texas: Digging for Secrets miniseries.

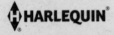

ISBN-13: 978-1-335-59481-5

Fortune in Name Only

Recycling programs
for this product may
not exist in your area.

Harlequin Enterprises ULC
22 Adelaide St. West, 41st Floor
Toronto, Ontario M5H 4E3, Canada
www.Harlequin.com

Printed in U.S.A.

A *USA TODAY* bestselling author of over 110 novels in twenty languages, **Tara Taylor Quinn** has sold more than seven million copies. Known for her intense emotional fiction, Ms. Quinn's novels have received critical acclaim in the UK and most recently from Harvard. She is the recipient of the Readers' Choice Award and has appeared often on local and national TV, including *CBS Sunday Morning*.

For TTQ offers, news and contests, visit www.tarataylorquinn.com!

Books by Tara Taylor Quinn

The Fortunes of Texas: Digging for Secrets

Fortune in Name Only

Harlequin Special Edition

Furever Yours

Love off the Leash

The Fortunes of Texas

Fortune's Christmas Baby

Sierra's Web

His Lost and Found Family
Reluctant Roommates
Her Best Friend's Baby
Their Secret Twins
Old Dogs, New Truths

Visit the Author Profile page at Harlequin.com for more titles.

For Luke Sorrell, my three-year-old farmer who, I feel sure, will one day own his own ranch.

Chapter One

"Ma'am, you can't mean that." Turning his charm on full power, Asa Fortune also injected huge amounts of sincere emotion into his gaze as he looked the widow in the eye. "I've just offered you a generous amount, more than you're asking for the place."

The woman liked him. Asa knew she did. He rented a cabin on the ranch, boarded his horse there. Helped her out around the place.

When she started to shake her head, he burst into words. "Mrs. Hensen, you've put fifty years of your life into the Chatelaine Dude Ranch. You and your husband raised your kids here. And you also, in a way, raised me," he admitted without a bit of shame. "I was here with my family when I was little, and it was one of the best times of my life. Because of those days, I became a rancher. I bought Majority right out of high school," he told her, naming the horse that he was currently boarding at the Chatelaine. "Together, we've traveled all over the state of Texas, working ranches, learning, preparing for this chance. I can promise you, there's no one you can trust more to carry on your legacy than Major and I."

All true, although he'd never believed his young boyhood dream of owning the Chatelaine Dude Ranch would ever come true. As an adult, he'd just been hoping to have his own ranch someday. And for the past twelve years, he'd worked tirelessly toward that goal.

Asa saw the flash of hope cross her face. He didn't imagine it. So it made no sense when she shook her head again.

Maybe he was the one missing something?

At an uncharacteristic loss for words, he watched the widow's mouth move and could barely comprehend what he was hearing.

"I've realized that I can't bear to sell the place to anyone who isn't married."

What? His brain started to sputter a flurry of responses, but she continued before he could articulate even one of them.

"This is a family ranch," she told him. "My heart breaks at the thought of it not going to a couple who will love it, invest their hearts in it together, like my husband and I did. There are tough days running a dude ranch," she continued. "Times when something goes wrong, and families need reassurance at the same time. And times when you're so busy, you're too exhausted, and you might want to quit, but then your spouse reminds you of the great days and suddenly you have energy again. And holidays…they're celebrated like family here, with owners who *are* a family and who understand the importance of family…"

"I understand the importance of family!" Asa burst out, interrupting her. Could he really be so close to sweet success and still fail? Lose a lifelong dream when he'd already mentally moved in? There were other bidders for the popular ranch, though he'd heard none were full price. Still, chances were good some were married. "Family is why I moved to Chatelaine last summer, right before you put up your For Sale sign! My relatives have been in Chatelaine for as long as you have! Many were born here. It's family inheritance money, from my great-uncle, that brought me here…"

She already knew most of what he was rambling on about. The whole town had heard about the letters the Fortune grandchildren had received from Freya Fortune, the previous summer, summoning them to Chatelaine to receive an inheritance they hadn't known existed.

Just as they hadn't been privy to the whereabouts of their disgraced uncle for years, or been aware that he'd married Freya.

Asa just couldn't be holding his dream in his arms and let it slip away. Not when he knew he could not only honor the Chatelaine legacy exactly as Val Hensen wanted but help the business grow and prosper for generations to come. "I not only see your and Mr. Hensen's vision for this place, I share it," he told her in an impassioned plea that was totally unlike himself.

When he saw a second shake of her head, his system went into total freeze mode. Unable to process what he was dealing with, or come up with a way to smile his way to victory, he blurted, "You can't just turn down the highest offer because of my marriage status."

And knew he'd made a grave mistake, turning the conversation adversarial, before he even registered the tightening of her expression.

"You come back here with that offer and a marriage license and we'll talk," the widow said in a less friendly tone. "For now, I'm taking the place off the market."

That first Monday in March was supposed to have been the day his life's dream came true. Instead, it was turning into a nightmare.

With those parting words, the widow shut the door in his face.

Lily Perry might have slowed her step as she saw Asa Fortune's truck turn onto Main Street right as she was deciding what to do on her break from work. The choice between heading to the bank and paying her electric bill, or stopping at the coffee shop was made for her when she saw him slow down. He might or might not head in for coffee himself, but if he was going to do so, she wanted to be there to hear his good news.

She'd been leaning toward the latter choice in any event. The bill wouldn't be late for another two days, which gave her a couple of more shifts at the café to earn tips. And maybe a chance to pay the bill without drawing on her somewhat limited savings account.

Not that anyone else in the world knew that piece of the puzzle. Both of her sisters, newly reunited with her, had the means, and, she was sure, the willingness to front her a loan if she ever needed it. But she'd die before asking.

Having provided fully for herself since she was seventeen years old, she knew how to make extra cash if she needed it. Had even driven a couple of towns over to clean house a time or two when she'd been strapped for cash.

Seeing Asa's truck slow just before the coffeehouse, all thoughts of personal cash flow flew the coop. The man had taken control of her senses since he'd moved to town the summer before. And while he'd dated seemingly every available female in Chatelaine except her, her heart still jumped at the chance to be the recipient of that magnetic smile.

And, maybe, secretly, it was also a bit thrilling to know that while Asa flitted from woman to woman, she was his one constant. The only female, according to him, who'd become a real friend to him.

Besides, he'd been going to make his dream come true that morning, and she couldn't wait to share his joy. He knew she'd understand. She'd told him about her personal connection to the dude ranch when he'd run into her and his sister Esme having coffee at the café at the GreatStore. She'd told him then how as a baby, she and her fellow-triplet sisters had spent the day at the dude ranch with their parents.

A few days after the coffee with Esme, she and Haley had run into him downtown, and when Lily told Haley then that Asa was buying the Chatelaine Dude Ranch, her sister had told him why that day at the ranch had meant so much to them. Those hours at the ranch had been the last ones they'd ever spent with their parents. Haley had told him what she knew about the one-car crash that had ripped their parents away from them that night, saying that she kept trying to find out more, but couldn't seem to.

Her sister had blurted out the story of old wounds that Lily didn't want to reopen. Ever.

But when Asa had looked at Lily, she'd teared up.

She would never forget the compassion that had filled his compelling brown eyes as he'd asked her how old she'd been.

Nor could she escape the memory of how she'd felt…comforted by his continued interest when she'd told him she'd only been ten months old. She'd quickly turned the subject back to him, in upbeat tones, telling him how she'd keep her fingers crossed for him to get the ranch that had always held such a special place in her heart.

Which was why it hadn't been a surprise to her when, a couple of days before, he'd stopped by the café at the GreatStore, to tell her he was making the new bid.

Wishing she was in something a little more sexy than her waitressing uniform, she opened the coffee-house door and waved at the people who glanced up, all of whom she knew. She had her usual smile on her freckled face as she ordered her usual—a hot chocolate—and took a seat at the only two-seater table left available. Her back deliberately to the door.

Which went against the grain for Lily in general. A girl who'd grown up with no real family, moving from one foster home to another, learned at a young age how to keep her own back covered. Even in a small town where everyone looked out for her.

The door opened. Was she the only one in the room not checking to see who'd come in?

If it was Asa, either he'd join her or he wouldn't. She'd be fine either way.

Grabbing her phone out of her pocket, Lily hoped it looked as though she'd just had a text buzz for her attention. Or some such thing.

And then, just as quickly, pocketed the device. *What was wrong with her?* She was a fully grown, twenty-nine-year-old, completely self-sufficient woman. Not a starry-eyed schoolgirl.

Not that she'd know it by the silly flutter her heart gave when she saw a cowboy boot fall into her line of vision. "Mind if I join you?"

The voice…it was his, but something about it wasn't right.

Forgetting herself, Lily's gaze shot immediately to

Asa's face. Noted the downturned lips, the flattened cheeks and more than that, the lack of a glint in his so sexy gaze.

"What's wrong?"

He looked like someone had died.

"Major's okay, right?" His horse was more family to him than any of the relatives he'd found when he'd arrived in town the year before.

Another thing they had in common—finding family in adulthood, rather than growing up with them. Though she'd known about her triplet sisters growing up, she'd had no idea where they were, and no money or way to find them. Turned out, Tabitha and Haley, who'd both had families, hadn't even known about her...

"He's fine." Setting his coffee on the table with a thump, Asa dropped to the chair across from her. Leaving her with no choice but to stare at his massive shoulders in the button-down shirt beneath his pouty face. Make that *gorgeous* pouty face.

"Your financing didn't work the way you wanted," she guessed then. While she didn't know the intimate details of his money, nor all that much about managing an inheritance of any size, let alone one as exorbitant as his, she'd known that he'd been overhauling his original purchase and investment budget. The Chatelaine ranch not only needed some updating, but he'd planned some additions, too.

A local horse training program for local children, being one of them.

When he shook his handsome, dark head, she

frowned. Then leaned in toward him, her worried gaze meeting his. "What then?"

"She turned me down."

"She *what*?!" Realizing she'd raised her voice with the force of her shock, she bent further in to practically whisper, "Why? How can she even do that? You were offering over asking price."

With a look of total disillusionment, he shrugged. "Says she'll only sell to a married buyer. Something about having had this epiphany about it being a family place, and she'll only feel good about it continuing that way if it's run by a married couple. She had her list of reasons."

"She can't do that, can she? Pick and choose a buyer based on someone's marital status?"

"I have no idea. And it doesn't matter. She's taking the place off the market rather than be forced to accept my bid."

Completely nonplussed, hurting for him, and quite a bit disappointed for herself, too, she stared at him in dismay. Ever since he'd told her he was upping his bid on the property, she'd been toying with the idea of offering to help him out as he took over at the dude ranch, just to give herself a valid excuse to spend time on the land she'd been on the last time she'd been with her parents.

Back when her life, her future, had seemed safe and secure.

When she'd had as many opportunities as her triplet sisters to make a great life for herself.

Not that her life wasn't great, it was. Just…

Asa's sad chuckle brought her mind straight back to him. "So, you want to marry me?" His eye roll told her how completely not serious the comment was.

She opened her mouth to offer a chuckle right back to him. A friend commiserating with a friend. And instead, what came out, with a burst of unfamiliar giddiness, was, "Okay."

"What?" Still wearing the smile that had accompanied his pathetic attempt at a laugh, Asa stared at Lily. As always, those hazel eyes captivated him. He'd never met a woman whose gaze always seemed to be telling him that she had something to say that he needed to hear.

But he had to have heard her wrong. Or her earnest expression was a cover for the laughter that would erupt as soon as he started to take her seriously.

Not that he felt much like being the butt of a joke at the moment. Even hers…

"Okay, I'll marry you."

Asa sat straight up. Fast. Cramming his shoulder blades into the back of the chair. Had the world gone mad?

Or the day just hadn't started yet, and he was caught in some kind of weird nightmare where he meets with a seller and isn't at all himself. And then gets proposed to by a woman who was probably his best friend in the world. If you could forge such a connection in the short time that he'd known her…

Taking a deep breath, he refrained from pinching himself to verify that, yes, he was really awake.

Watching Lily, seeing her fidget, and noting how her freckles were growing more pronounced with the color forming on her cheeks, he took a sip of his coffee that turned out to be a gulp. Of steaming hot liquid.

Which burned the hell out of his tongue.

Yep, he was definitely conscious.

"You can't be serious," he said then. Enough time had passed to ensure that she wasn't about to burst into laughter.

"Why not?" She shrugged. The color on her cheeks intensified even more. Those freckles had become frequent visitors in his dreams. He loved how they gave him clues into Lily's thoughts. Or emotions.

How they set her apart. Like there was more to hanging out with her than with any other woman.

When he was done with his freckle obsession, he started to silently compile the dozens of reasons "why not."

"How about if, while you figure out all the why-nots, I tell you why?" Her voice hit him softly…but with the power of a ton of bricks. So much so that he nodded.

But didn't look away. Because for the first time since Mrs. Hensen had shut that door in his face, Asa was feeling something besides despair.

Of course, he knew there was no way he could ever marry Lily Perry. First, because he wasn't marrying *anyone*. But definitely not the one person in the world he wanted to have in his life forever. In his experience, based not only on his parents, but his aunt and uncle, too, marriage and real life didn't exist well together. Instead, the recipe created rancor, resentment, tension, eventual affairs...

She'd given him a second to stop her.

He waited instead. Expecting her to retreat. If there was one thing he'd learned about Lily that he wished was different, it was the way she always settled for what she had, rather than reaching for more.

He understood. Her life hadn't been easy. He admired the hell out of the way she always found the good in things. And was secretly addicted to her perennial sunny mood. But she could do both. Find good and reach for more...

"For starters, I'm in kind of a slump." If he hadn't been seated, her words would have floored him. Had the woman read his mind? Using what he'd just thought about her against him?

Or was it for him? The morning was just getting too bizarre.

If he didn't know better, he'd think he'd been drinking.

"Ever since I reconnected with my sisters... I look at them, my triplets, who started out in the same womb with me, and now one is a mother of twin babies, the other a successful magazine writer, and me? I'm refilling cups and ketchup dispensers..." Seeing the shrug of her slim shoulders, with that long dark hair gracing them, hit him hard.

For no reason he could understand.

Then her mouth quirked, and she gave a little head tilt, admitting softly, "Truth is, I already had a plan to ask you, once the place was officially yours, if I could come help out, work for you, as you took over the business."

He had a feeling he knew where she was going with this but didn't want to make any assumptions, so he gestured for her to go on.

"I know it might sound a bit over the top, but I want to be able to have a good reason to spend time out there. I told you before I've always had a fondness for the ranch. It's the last place I was before I became an orphan in the foster system. You know? The last time I was a member of my own family." She shrugged again. Looked away.

"It's not out there. I get it." Asa forced himself to ignore the temptation to reach for her hand. Lily was off-limits. Sacred. She was a…friend. "But—"

"It wouldn't have to be for long," she said then, glancing back over at him.

She wasn't letting it go.

Not allowing *him* to let it go.

"Once the place is in your name…it would probably behoove us to, you know, stay together for a while."

"A while, huh?" he couldn't keep himself from asking. "Exactly how long are you thinking?"

"Just long enough to make it look like we tried… but think about it, Asa. Who on earth would ever believe that a woman like me—the perennial friend— would ever be able to keep a hunk like you satisfied?"

He saw no pain or mockery in her grin. Just the

wide-open honesty that had drawn him to her from the first time they'd met.

But his own anger made up for her lack thereof. Leaning forward, he gave himself time for a deep breath and then gritted out, "Don't you ever, *ever* say anything like that again," he said softly. "You are worthy of the best man on earth, Lily Perry. It's the men who aren't worthy of you."

Her lips trembled. And she glanced away. He wasn't sure she believed him.

He meant the words with every fiber of his being.

Himself included.

If only there was a way he could make certain that he and Lily would never fight for real, never fester any resentment...

But, wait.

"You really planned to ask me to come work at the ranch?"

"It would be lot more challenging than delivering plated burgers."

"If we did this, and it's a big *if,* I'd be the one at fault when we separate. In some big obvious way..." What was he saying? *Thinking?*

Was he really considering this outrageous scheme?

Her nod seemed a bit...jerky. Had he scared her?

Talking like he was really going to consider the ludicrous idea?

"Rest assured," he quickly added, "there'd be separate bedrooms."

He saw her flinch that time, then noted her chin lift as she said, "I didn't see it happening any other way."

He almost grinned at her tone of voice. The woman might not ask much for herself, but she could most definitely hold her own.

Against anyone.

Him included.

Sitting back in his chair, he exhaled slowly, then locked eyes with her once again. "I need to think about it," he told her.

Her nod was circumspect.

But the smile that lit her face was something Asa knew he was never going to forget.

For better or worse.

Chapter Two

Had she lost total sight of reality? Taking Asa's facetiousness seriously? She'd known he was kidding. Lily would be the last woman he'd ask to marry him.

If he even *had* marriage on the radar. As his best friend—she knew he didn't. His comments on the subject had been few, but he'd made it clear that he thought marriage was a risk not worth taking anytime in the semi-near future. That the institution put people into a position of being forced to deal with hard stuff together, which ultimately ended up turning love into...well...disdain. At the very least.

But...he was *thinking* about getting hitched?

Lily knew the thought of marrying Asa should scare her a little. Especially considering his comment about separate bedrooms. She was in love with the man. How could she live with him platonically even for one night—let alone however long their marriage lasted—without giving herself away? Or dying of want?

But if he was seriously considering the idea… Sighing, she watched him sip his coffee. Lily had no idea if he was thinking about the proposal right then, weighing pros and cons while he sat with her, or just waiting for her to finish her hot chocolate and get back to work—leaving him in peace.

For all she knew he was at the coffee shop to meet someone else.

A woman, perhaps, who could be walking in at any moment.

Still, just in case he *was* actually contemplating a marriage between the two of them, she did the same. Her whole life, she'd felt as though the only family she had was the town. The people, collectively. Her dream had always been to get married, have a home and family of her very own.

So yeah, maybe, as her sisters both claimed, she settled for less than she deserved. But a marriage of convenience, the chance to call the Chatelaine Dude Ranch home, to actually *live* there, in the same house as the man she loved, while being instrumental in making his own dream come true… No way she'd give up that chance. Even if it wasn't a real marriage.

At least she'd be taking the first step toward her own wished-for destiny. She'd have the marriage and the home for a while. And when the marriage ended, she'd still have the memory. She'd know what it felt like to be happy. And she'd be closer to having it for real one day because she'd finally have reached out for something she wanted. And had gotten it…albeit temporarily.

The clock ticked. Asa sipped his coffee. Watching her. Opening his mouth, then closing it again.

She had to get back to work.

As if reading her mind, Asa stood. Nodded at her. "You need to think about it, too," he told her, as if they hadn't just sat there with a good two minutes of silence between them.

"I don't need to think about it," she responded without hesitation, standing as well. Heading out the door with him and then into the bright sun, she turned to face him on the sidewalk. "I'm in for the reasons I've already told you."

And for the one she hadn't. The one he'd never know. That she was in love with him.

Because she didn't kid herself for a second that her living with Asa, then appearing as a real husband and wife to the town, would suddenly make him fall for her. If she had that hope, she'd run for the hills. She might not reach for things out of her grasp, but she most definitely watched out for herself and avoided known danger at all cost.

And thinking that Asa Fortune would fall for a simple, plain woman like her would be dangerous. She wasn't sexy, or glam, and her hair would always hang around her shoulders in a way that could never be considered amazing…

Yet at this moment, he was staring at her as if she

was someone special, and her entire being warmed from the inside out.

"I can't believe you'd do this for me."

"I'm doing it for me, too," she reminded him softly. "Have you seen my place?" She nodded toward the part of town where she rented a tiny apartment. "Trading that for even one room at the Chatelaine Dude Ranch…" She shook her head. "No comparison."

She was making light of the changes her life would take. And the fact that they were only temporary. She knew and could tell he did, too.

Still…she thrummed with an energy, an excitement she'd never known.

Pulling her over toward the brick wall of the building, away from the middle of the sidewalk, he murmured, "We'd probably only have to stay married for like six months." He said it as though offering good news.

She nodded.

"You're seriously okay with this?" His gaze bore into hers.

She withstood the look without a blink. "I am."

His hand shot out toward her, and when she didn't react, he reached for hers. "It's a deal," he said, grasping her hand in the bigger, warm palm of his. And then he pulled her toward him, drawing her right up against the hardness of his body, and gave her a hug.

A bear hug. A *friendly* hug.

Yet it was the first time her body had ever touched

his, full-on. And desire made Lily so weak, she had to hold on.

Tight.

Asa was not a man who fooled around. Or wasted time. He never had been. He was a man driven to reach his goals…who strove to make his life the best it could be. A man who was dedicated to working hard every single day and who wasn't afraid to dream big.

Knowing that he was maybe a bit over-the-top on all of that, some might call him pushy, didn't stop him from barreling ahead when he saw the path in front of him.

From his rented cabin on the Chatelaine Dude Ranch—his home since he'd arrived in Chatelaine in response to the inheritance letter he'd received the summer before—Asa called Lily that night. A quick reach out, begun and done in a matter of seconds, just to make certain she was fully on board with their plan. And to offer her more time, if she needed it.

With her go-ahead clear, he was up early the next morning. His first order of business was to drive directly to the jewelers as soon as they opened. He had to tend to every aspect of the plan, make it appear real, so Widow Hensen would be convinced. And legally, the marriage would be real.

His next stop was his lawyer's office. To have a prenuptial agreement drawn up, giving Lily a sizable amount of his net worth once the marriage was dissolved.

No way he was reaching for his own dream, changing his life forever, without equally changing hers. For the good.

She'd have no need to ever go back to the café or her rented apartment. She'd have the chance to do what she wanted to do for a living.

The marriage wouldn't last, but as far as he was concerned, the bond between them and the benefits the marriage brought most definitely would.

He knew she was working that day, and that shifts ended at four. A busy time at the GreatStore in which the café was located.

Dressed in new black jeans, shined black cowboy boots, a white button-down shirt, and leaving his Stetson on the seat of his truck, he entered the building at fifteen minutes before the hour.

He'd thought he'd mosey some, be casual, but as it occurred to him that she could have plans and run out as soon as she was off, he made a beeline straight for the café. And stood there, all dressed up, getting a few interested looks and a smile from a woman he'd dated a time or two the previous fall. A guy he knew from the ranch was heading down the main aisle of the store, right for him. While he was glad to have the chance at a firsthand witness to what was about to happen, most likely on its way straight to Val Hensen, no way he wanted to be stuck in conversation with another cowboy when Lily appeared.

Nothing left to do but head into the café and seek her out, even while she was still on the clock. He'd planned on waiting till her shift ended to do this, but now those plans had changed. Besides, it wasn't like she needed the job anymore. If he had any sway with her, she'd be quitting that day. She'd told him more than once that while she loved seeing the people who came in, loved being around town folk every day, she hated the work. It bored her.

If they were entering into a real marriage, he'd know he'd have some sway.

With that thought at the top of his mind, Asa saw Lily exit the café's kitchen, a filled salad bowl in hand, and head to a table.

He headed toward her.

Seconds later, he was a couple of feet up the aisle, blocking her way when she turned back toward the kitchen. Everyone seemed to be staring at him. He *hoped* they were at least, as he bent down on one knee, pulled the newly purchased ring box out of his pocket and opened it to show the glistening two-carat diamond he'd picked out that morning.

He heard gasps.

Only then did he look up at the woman he'd virtually trapped between tables and any exit. "Lily Perry, would you do me the honor of marrying me?"

His gaze was only for her. Steady. Letting her know, that she had every right to turn him down and he wouldn't hold it against her if she did, while at the same time, trying to look the besotted lover to all of his inadvertent witnesses.

The way Lily's mouth fell open helped his plan.

The doubt he thought he saw flash in her eyes, not so much.

She recovered quickly. Pasted a smile on her face. Followed by the light a normal fiancée would expect to see in his betrothed eyes. He'd known Lily was a great friend. An incredible person. However, he'd never known she was such a good actress.

"Yes." Her voice trembled, caught, so much in fact that he wasn't sure he'd heard the right answer.

Until clapping and whoops broke out around them. Thanking fates for the startling cacophony that was his clue to actually pull the ring out of the box, he grabbed Lily's left hand, and glided the ring on her second to last finger.

Shocked again, as a curious thrill spread through him as the ring slid home.

He knew why…because he was getting the ranch.

Asa just hadn't expected such an emotional reaction from himself. Wasn't sure what to do next. How far did he take a fake proposal?

They hadn't exactly discussed how it would all unfold.

Letting go of Lily's hand as he panicked for a second, disgusted by his lack of preparedness, he felt Lily's fingers close around his. Holding on to him as she pulled him up to his feet.

And into her body.

Sliding her arms around him, she held on tight.

Lifted her face to smile at him.

And he did the stupidest thing he'd done in… maybe ever.

He lowered his head and kissed her.

* * *

Lily had almost backed out.

She should have said no.

And despite everything, she couldn't help the surge of sadness inside her as Asa's lips touched hers to the sounds of whoops and hollers and whistles. In front of friends and coworkers, whom she considered to be her family, she was living her greatest dream come true. Except that where it counted, in the heart of hearts, it was all fake.

The feel of those lips, though, the warmth, wiped out everything but Asa. Her mouth opened to him, and for a second, she forgot their audience. And their pretense. She kissed him back with passion, and when he pulled back, and she saw the thankfulness in his gaze as he looked only at her, she knew that she'd walk to the end of the earth for the man.

What was six months of her life to make his future right? Six months where she got to live a portion of her own greatest desires? Part was better than *nothing*, after all.

With that thought solidifying her choice, knowing that there was no backing out for her, she kissed him once more, just for the heck of it. And then, stepping back, she took a moment to smile at everyone coming forward to express their shock and delight, before she left Asa to deal with the scene he'd made and went to clock out.

Asa waited for Lily. A guy didn't just propose and then leave. Not him, at any rate. Accepting the well-wishes of a few people he knew, and more who'd known Lily her entire life whom he'd never met, he kept watch for his brand-new fiancée.

Only then fully grasping what he'd just done. What he'd gotten them both into.

If he hadn't been so worried that Widow Hensen would put the ranch back on the market and find a married buyer willing to offer more than asking price, selling it right out from under him, he might have had the sense to slow down.

To talk over parameters with Lily, at the very least.

He knew they weren't just entering into a platonic, limited time marriage for Val Hensen's sake. They were embarking on a union that everyone would think was real.

Chatelaine was an old-fashioned small town that wasn't progressive like other communities in Texas. The people there wanted things left just like they were.

And they were *not* the type of folks who'd likely look kindly on a man using one of their own to his own gain.

Feeling like a lout, he kept a smile on his face and grabbed Lily's hand as soon as, purse in hand, she reappeared from the back room.

"We need to talk," he whispered directly into her ear.

Even if she had other pressing plans, she'd have to change them.

His fault.

He'd make it up to her.

But if he'd just sent a boulder down a hill to crash her world into pieces, he had to find a way to stop the descent.

She was busy accepting well-wishes and being stopped for hugs as they made their way out of the café. But she seemed as eager as he was to be alone.

To sort out the mess he'd made.

And, if they were going forward, to get plans in place for future public appearances.

He wanted his future.

But *not* at the cost of hers.

As he pushed through the door of the GreatStore, holding it for her, he could feel the sweat trickling down his back and promised himself he'd just made his last mistake where Lily Perry was concerned.

Chapter Three

We need to talk.

That kind of lead-in usually meant the conversation would not be good.

They'd reached the GreatStore parking lot.

Asa started talking. "We can take my truck, maybe head out to my cabin at the ranch. Word getting to Val Hensen that we're alone there together would be good, but we'd also have plenty of privacy."

And they'd be at the ranch. Their whole reason for getting married.

"I can't, Asa. Not right this second. I'm meeting my sisters for an early dinner." True. Though she didn't have to show up at the restaurant for another hour. She just wasn't ready for "the talk." Not ten minutes after he'd shocked her with the impromptu and incredibly romantic proposal in front of a crowd of people who'd known her all her life.

She'd needed it to be real in the worst way.

But it wasn't. And she had to get a grip on that before things went any further. So right now, with the way her body was humming and her heart was crying, being alone with him at his cabin was a *very* bad idea.

"Call them," he said, pulling her down out of the way of the store's entrance. "Make it an hour later, and I'll take us all out to the LC Club."

He said it as though visiting the ritzy oasis set twenty miles out of town with multiple balcony dining spaces overlooking Lake Chatelaine, wasn't a once-in-a-lifetime experience. For Tabitha, it wouldn't be. Probably not for Haley, either. But for Lily?

She'd never been.

And didn't want her first time to be a fake celebration. Most particularly not when she'd be there with the three people she loved most in the world.

Shaking her head, Lily pulled away from Asa. Secretly hating the way his brows drew together, like he was pained, but held her ground, just the same.

"My time with my sisters…it's still kind of sacrosanct to me. You know, having grown up without knowing them… I can meet you after," she said to him. "We can drive out to the lake, if you'd like."

We need to talk purported a need for privacy, and it wasn't like they could find that at the LC Club.

As soon as she saw his nod, she turned toward the employee parking area and was further put out when

Asa kept in step beside her, until he murmured, "Just to keep up appearances."

At which point she nodded, grinned at him, and walked fast.

She still felt like she was racing as she sat, in newly donned jeans and a short-sleeved shirt, fork suspended over her chef salad, facing her triplet sisters an hour later.

It was like she couldn't catch her breath. Had been that way since she'd seen Asa down on his knee in front of her, holding out that ridiculously fancy diamond ring.

She'd taken it off the second she'd shut herself in her old beater of a car.

"Tell us already," Haley said, sounding more caring than exasperated. Lily saw the glance she shared with Tabitha, the beautiful blonde sister, as Lily thought of her. One more suited to Asa Fortune, for sure, if not for the fact that Tabitha had already loved, and lost, a Fortune. Weston Fortune's death had left her a single mother, raising their year-old twins alone.

"Tell you what?" Lily knew pretending was only going to stall the inevitable. When pretense had gotten her into this whole mess to begin with. And besides, she'd needed to talk to her sisters.

But just putting it out there…facing reality. Was she really ready for that? A part of her wanted to cling to fantasy for a second or two longer.

"We both got calls," Tabitha said softly, her blond

hair falling perfectly against the sides of her face, her green eyes filled with questions.

"Within a minute of him asking," Haley confirmed.

"You knew we would." Tabitha again.

And Lily put her fork down.

"Trouble is, you aren't wearing the ring." Haley just kept coming at her. "And you sure don't look like an ecstatic, newly engaged woman."

"Which, considering how besotted you are with the guy, is a bit of a concern," Tabitha added.

They weren't going to let this go. And truthfully, she didn't want them to. She just wished, for once, she wasn't the poor fledging among them. The one who didn't have a life mapped out in front of her.

Because who else would enter into a fake marriage just to help out a friend?

"It's a favor," she leaned in to say. There. She'd put it out there. Quietly. Just between the three of them. And effectively ended the weird flight into make believe she'd been teetering around in. "But before I tell you any more, I need you both to swear that this goes no further," she said, looking between the two of them with a solid gaze.

Both women nodded immediately.

"I mean it," she reiterated. "No one." If word got out, the adventure was over. And Asa lost everything he most desired.

"Of course," Tabitha agreed.

"Goes without saying," Haley said. "We're our safe place, right?" Her glance encompassed Lily and Tabitha equally.

"Right," they both answered solemnly. In tandem.

As though they'd grown up together rather than just being part of the same birthing event, and sharing a home for the first ten months of their lives.

"So yeah, I'm a fool," Lily said with a beleaguered sigh, suddenly feeling a lot younger than her sisters despite the fact that they were all the same age. But looking over at Tabitha, the doting mother, and Haley, the incredibly talented magazine writer, she suddenly just knew. She wasn't going to change her mind.

No matter the eventual cost to her heart.

"What have you two been telling me for the past year?"

"That you need to expect more out of life," Haley answered first.

"That you deserve more than you allow yourself to expect," Tabitha chimed in with her version of the same.

"Right. Well, um, as it turns out, Asa can't buy the ranch unless he's married. So…"

"He asked you to marry him, to give up your life, so he can buy a *ranch*?"

Not a ranch. *The ranch.* "No. He made a joke. I'm the one who talked him into it."

"Still…he's letting you give up your life for…"

She shook her head before Haley could finish the sentence. "No," she stated emphatically. "First, I'm not giving up my life. The marriage is only temporary. Second, it's in name only, though as far as the town is concerned, it will be real. Basically, I'm moving from my apartment to the main house on the ranch for the next six months or so…" Assuming Asa's *talk* didn't change that.

"Ah, Lil…" Tabitha's look was full of…worry. "You love him. You think you'll share his daily life for six months and then just be able to walk away?"

Shoulders straight, she shot back, "What I think is that I'm reaching for what I want," she told them pointedly. "I want a home. Marriage. I want to be surrounded by family. And while this isn't at all what I'd envisioned, it's a hell of a lot better than waitressing at the café."

Both women kept their mouths shut, but their facial features expressed their doubts loud and clear.

"Sharing his life for six months is better than not ever having known what living with him is like," she continued, articulating thoughts she hadn't fully landed on yet. "Who knows, maybe Asa will turn out to be no fun at all in everyday life."

"And if he's everything you ever hoped for?" Haley asked again.

"Then I know what to reach for. Don't you see? You both grew up in a regular homes. You've had stability your entire lives. I never have. Besides, love isn't about what you get, it's what you give. I'm helping Asa's dream come true…"

"And when the marriage is over…you move back to your apartment, or one like it, and go back to work at the café?" Tabitha asked the question, but it blared from Haley's expression as well.

"No." She was never going back. To either. "I expect that Asa will keep me employed at the ranch for as long as I want to be…" Assuming she made it there at all.

As minutes passed, Lily grew more and more anxious about that talk Asa had said they had to have. Surely, he wouldn't make a big public proposal and two minutes later cut her off.

He wanted the ranch too badly to do that, the more practical side of her reminded herself.

"I told him, when I was giving him my reasons for wanting to help him, that I'd already been planning to ask him for a job as soon as he got the ranch…"

Ignoring the salad in front of her…her stomach was too knotted to eat much…Lily nibbled on a dinner roll as she gave her sisters a rundown of the reasons she'd used to convince Asa to marry her. Ending with… "And the bottom line is…I want to do this," she told them both. "It might be dumb, I might get hurt, but at least I'm daring to live bigger…"

When Haley and Tabitha both nodded, Lily's stomach settled some. She might be walking into heartache, but she was doing so consciously, by her own choice.

"And who knows," Tabitha said, sharing a glance, and a small smile, with her triplets. "Maybe he'll fall in love, too, and the marriage will become real."

Haley's brows raised, her eyes wide, and, glancing at Lily, she added, "I can't imagine any straight man living with Lily for six weeks, let alone six months, without falling for her…"

Lily got that her sisters were trying to make her

feel better. But she'd been residing in a town that was full of eligible men her entire life and not one of them had ever tried to snatch her up.

And it didn't matter, because the last thing she needed was false hope.

What she *did* need, however, was to get out of there, call Asa, and get every second of living she could out of the next six months.

Asa almost didn't pick up when Lily's call came through. From practically the minute he'd left her at her car in the GreatStore parking lot, he'd been getting calls from his siblings and cousins, congratulating him. He'd wanted word to travel fast. He'd just never expected the deluge that rained down upon him.

But then, he was still reeling somewhat from the huge changes life had brought him. A decades old mining tragedy that had driven his grandfather and great uncle out of town, after they'd pinned the blame on someone else, had turned into a windfall for their heirs Asa had been shocked when he'd received the letter telling him that he was the beneficiary of a fairly large sum of money. Even then, he'd never, in a million years, expected that the family members he'd never met would welcome him home as if he'd lived there all his life.

Turned out his Fortune cousins were so much in his life that they'd been noticing how much Asa and Lily hung out together and had been hoping that he'd be bringing another one of the Perry triplets into the family.

While Tabitha wasn't officially a Fortune, with West, a former federal prosecutor, having been killed before they'd been married—before he'd even known he was going to be a father—her twins were most definitely carrying Fortune blood, and the entire clan had welcomed Tabitha in as one of them.

And his own sisters…well, they'd been giddy over the idea of him actually getting over their rancorous upbringing and settling down.

Which, of course, wasn't happening at all.

Still feeling the sting of guilt over keeping the truth to himself about his impending nuptials to Lily, he'd glanced at his ringing phone on the fourth ring and saw that it was his bride-to-be.

"Hey!" he answered, anticipation replacing all of the other emotions that had been rolling around inside him. "I thought you'd be another hour or so…"

"I can meet up with you later, if you're busy."

"Now's just fine," he told her, arranging to pick her up at her place in five minutes. And as he hung up, he couldn't help feeling relieved that she was back to her easygoing, accommodating self.

Not that he wanted her to always let him have his way. On the contrary, he'd like to show her, during their time together, that she didn't always have to fit into everyone else's plans. Just like earlier, outside the store, when she'd turned down his dinner invitation.

She could say no, and it wouldn't change anything between them.

In fact, he wanted her to feel comfortable asking for what she wanted from *him*, and he'd do his best to give it to her.

That thought in mind, as soon as she climbed into his truck, he said, "I want this marriage to be a two-way street." No hello. Just him, pushing forward into his future.

Which was now hers, as well, at least for a time.

"You're the one friend in the world I think I've ever wholly trusted, Lily, and I don't want anything to ever jeopardize that."

What the hell was he doing?

"What's going to jeopardize it?" she asked, looking cute and comfortable in her jeans and shirt. No makeup, hair just flowing naturally. That was Lily.

And he wouldn't have her any other way.

"You not benefiting in a big way from it as well."

He'd intended to wait until they were parked at the lake to get into it with her. Had planned to take Major out for half an hour before he met up with her again, too.

To have some soul-calming family time.

He told her about his conversations with his lawyer. The prenuptial agreement he'd already had drawn up.

"That's ridiculous, Asa, you don't have to do that."

Glancing over at her, he pulled off onto a dirt road, parked by some trees, and turned to her. "This marriage is changing my life forever, Lily, giving me my future. It needs to do the same for you. No way you just go back to working at the café, not unless you loved the work, and remember, this is me? I already know you don't. You love seeing the people, being a part of their lives, every day, being able to keep up on everyone's news. But the work…"

Her smile was more self-deprecatory than filled with humor as she conceded the point with a nod. They'd had a long talk over beers one night about their jobs. Him needing to move on from ranch hand to ranch owner. And her not knowing what she'd move on to.

"I don't want to be bought." Her words were barely above a whisper. He felt them to his core.

"Are you marrying me for money?" He met her gaze in the early evening, shaded sun glow.

"Of course not! How could you even ask that?" Her hazel eyes glared at him, like pinpricks of gold and steel.

"Then you aren't being bought." He waited a second for his words to settle over her before continuing. "You're working toward your future," he told her. "You want a home of your own. You said so. That's one of your dreams to the point that you're willing to settle for six months of having one, rather than never having the chance." He huffed out a breath. "But I can't do that to you. Just let you taste your dream and then snatch it away. You're doing this to make me happy, well, I need to make you happy, too. When we get married, you'll be getting a home for life. For the first six months, or so, you'll be sharing mine. After that, you'll have the resources to choose one you want."

Saying the words aloud, knowing she was hearing them, settled some of the qualms inside him. "It's the only way I can do this," he told her, holding her gaze tightly. "This arrangement can't be a one-way thing."

She didn't look away. Lily wasn't a wallflower. She didn't hide. She just...*expected less than she deserved*. Words she'd told him months ago, again over beers, repeating what her sister, the mother of his second cousins, had said to her.

When she nodded, she didn't look happy, but she didn't seem upset, either. She seemed to have lost, or at least fully contained, all of the agitation his impromptu proposal had raised in her.

"About this afternoon," he began, glancing at the diamond he'd placed on her finger, liking the way it glistened there, "I'm sorry for the way that went down. I was..."

"Being you," she said, with a real grin. "Getting the job done."

"Yeah." He grinned back. "But I could have let you in on the plan ahead of time," he allowed.

"Might have been a good idea."

"So...we're good?" he asked.

"Yep."

He gazed at her fondly. "You know I love ya, right?"

"I figured, maybe."

"You want to get a beer?"

When her usual positive response didn't immediately follow, Asa's gut tightened again.

"I just…if Widow Hensen suspects that this marriage isn't real…you still won't get the ranch," Lily reminded him.

"I know." He figured that went without saying, literally. "The whole point of the proposal was…"

He stopped when he saw her frown. "What?" he asked.

"In public, Asa…we're going to have to act like it's real. Holding hands. Sitting next to each other at the table, having conversations with our heads close together sometimes…"

He'd had the same thoughts but was trying not to dwell on them too much.

"You have a problem with that?" he asked her.

"No."

"So…you want to get that beer?"

Her smile was still lighting him up inside as he parked outside the Corral, the popular rancher bar just outside of town, where they'd met the previous summer. Aafter exiting the truck, he reached for her hand.

He felt her softer palm and fingers intermingle with his calloused ones. Didn't hate it.

Two friends, lifting each other to their futures.

Life had never been better.

Chapter Four

Lily put her notice in the next day at work, but agreed to work a few more days, just until management could fill her schedule. She could pretend that life was going on as normal—other than the huge rock surrounded by a setting of smaller ones she was carrying around on her left ring finger—except that nothing about the following couple of days felt at all normal.

Everyone who saw her in the café either congratulated her or asked about a wedding date. Her sisters were both calling daily to check up on her—and wanting to know the same.

Plus every single one of the Fortune cousins currently in town, and Asa's two sisters, had called, or stopped by to welcome her to the family—all of them offering to help with wedding plans. And it got to the point that on Friday, after work, she had to take matters into her own hands. Her last day at the café had culminated with a surprise shower for her, gifts consisting of things she'd need for a wedding, like certificates for a manicure and pedicure, a waxing—like she'd have any reason to need that—a hair appointment, and a pile of gift certificates for the GreatStore.

She and Asa had been meeting in town for dinner each night, usually at the Chatelaine Bar & Grill, the nicest place in town, to be seen as much as to eat, and she started in on him as soon as she joined him in the red-leather booth.

Rather than asking if he'd been waiting long—she'd been late due to more well-wishers stopping her as she tried to get out of the café—she slid onto the chair directly across from him and started right in. "I think we need to get this over and done with," she told him. "Let's just go to Town Hall and get married." She could use the gift certificates making her purse bulge as Christmas gifts or something.

Asa quirked a brow. "Right now?"

"Probably best to wait for them to open, but Monday morning, for sure. People can throw whatever parties they want to for us afterward. Or we can have a big housewarming at the ranch once the closing happens."

His glance at her seemed a little worried. And she sighed. "I've just spent twenty minutes trying to get a word in edgewise with my sisters, regarding me having a dress suitable for marrying a Fortune. Tabitha wants me to wear the wedding dress she had made to marry West, but never got to wear. If we don't get this done, we're going to have one-year-old twin ring bearers and a magazine spread of the big day, too."

Her sisters, bless their hearts, were trying to make everything so real and perfect in the hope that Asa was going to fall in love with her—not just love her as a friend. In the hopes that the marriage would turn out to be real. And by then the wedding would already have happened, robbing Lily, in their opinion, of the chance to have her big day. And pictures and memories to cherish forever. They wanted to make sure she had that.

Didn't matter how many times she told them that she didn't care about that kind of stuff.

Asa suddenly pulling out his phone, as though her conversation wasn't worthy of his attention, didn't sit well, either. Not right then, after a busy day at work, and too much pressure coming at her.

For a second there, she wished herself back to the nonentity life she felt like she'd lived since she was ten months old. Invisible, or slightly visible, under the radar at least, wasn't all bad.

Not wanting to chance anyone witnessing a cross word from her to him, she picked up the menu as though she'd hadn't just read it the night before. And wished they were over at the Corral, having wings and chips. At least there the conversation was louder and the mood lighter.

"There's a seventy-two-hour waiting period after you apply for the license until you can get married."

She glanced across the booth at her pseudo fiancé. He'd been reading about getting married? Not finding something more important than her wedding woes on his phone?

And of less importance, but easier to deal with in the moment, "We have to wait until next Thursday to do this? That's like…almost another whole week from now!"

Another week in which Val Hensen could find some married person to buy the Chatelaine Dude Ranch. Asa would lose his chance. And she…really and truly wanted her chance, too. She wanted to marry the man, to make the deal, to change her life, build her future into something more than her past had been. If they had to wait, they had to wait, but it was going to be a very nerve-wracking week on so many levels.

He leaned in toward her. "Let's go to Vegas."

Heart jumping, she stared at him. Saw the seriousness in his gaze. And a new light there, too.

"Vegas?" She didn't squeak, but almost. "I've never been outside of Texas." In fact, she'd never been more than a hundred miles from Chatelaine. Excitement pumped through her. "Is it like you see on those old CSI, Las Vegas reruns?"

"Pretty much," he told her. "Though we can stay off the strip if you'd like. They have marriage chapels around the town."

"No!" She blurted so loud, one of the managers from The GreatStore, who was seated with his wife at the table next to them, glanced over. "I want to go!" she finished, not much quieter. "I want to see it all."

And a fake wedding where she had her groom all to herself…the groom she loved for real…sounded better than anything she'd ever dared dream up for herself. There'd be no worrying about what other people saw, or thought. No pretending. Just a woman eloping with her best friend, knowing that he wasn't going to have sex with her.

Just her and Asa on the most incredible road trip…

He talked to her about wedding venue options, looked up flights, and booked them two seats for Sunday morning, then moved on to hotels. Eventually choosing what he said was one of the most opulent, in the best part of the strip, he got them the honeymoon suite plus. The plus part was that in addition to the lavish master suite, the accommodations included a second, smaller bedroom. For her, she assumed. Which was what she preferred anyway. No way she wanted to sleep alone in a big romantic wedding room bed.

Of course, for show, they'd be able to bring back photos of the amenities, including a heart-shaped bed, chocolate-covered strawberries, and exclusive champagne.

It was working out perfectly. In a way, she was getting the wedding of her dreams. Just her and Asa, all alone, on a magical trip, in Sin City, staying in a room that would surely feel like paradise to her. For those two days and one night, she'd be a princess. And he'd be her prince.

Grown-up version, of course.

And not having to go through a wedding in Chatelaine, where everyone would be watching, where her sisters would be looking on, knowingly, where she'd worry every second that someone would call them on the pretense...that relief was palpable.

Lily was still flying high as she and Asa left the restaurant, their plans all firmly settled. So much so that she slid her hand behind his elbow and down, linking her arm with his. He stiffened, but then immediately relaxed, hugging her arm close to him, and she couldn't help thinking what a perfect moment it was.

Right up until they started down the sidewalk to their vehicles and Baylor Minser turned a corner and started toward them. The tall, thin, glamorous blonde with her perfect make up and long, flowing, flawlessly styled hair was one of the women Asa took out on occasion.

Had he called her? Let her know the marriage was a fake?

Even as Lily had the thought, she was admonishing herself. Asa wouldn't do that to Lily. Or risk sabotaging his chances of getting the ranch, either.

Smile, just keep walking, get past her, Lily was saying to herself.

"Asa! Hello!" Baylor called out, as though just then noticing them. The woman's gaze was firmly on Asa, her smile inviting more than just words, even as she said, "I hear congratulations are in order..."

At which point Baylor gave a quick up-and-down glance over Lily. With a smirk filled with disdain before turning her gaze, accompanied by a bright smile, right back on Asa. "I wish I'd known you were in the market for more than a good time," she said, with a little pout. "I'm sure we could have worked something out..."

She let her words trail off as she passed them—on Asa's side—making sure that the side of her hand grazed his thigh as she did so.

Lily couldn't say how Asa reacted. She was too busy trying to keep her own despair firmly under wraps. Clearly, whether her marriage to the handsome cowboy was real or not, there were some women who were still going to be available to him.

And...

"I need you to promise me something," she blurted, all sense of euphoria giving way to panic. But at least she had her feet firmly back in her own world where they belonged.

"What?" Asa didn't seem the least bit different. As though seeing Baylor had had no effect on him at all. Good or bad.

Because he knew he'd be calling her for a little *on the side* action the woman had made clear she'd still be willing to offer?

"I know our marriage is pretense, and this is asking a lot of a guy like you, but I can't do this if I'm going to be humiliated."

"A guy like me?" He was still walking...still holding her arm. But more loosely. And his tone had a more distant edge to it, too.

"You're sexy, Asa. Virile. You have healthy desires and places to assuage them..." What the hell.

She was going to start spouting like some kind of virginal heroine of a melodrama now? "I just…you need to promise me it won't be in this town. Or with anyone who lives here. Not as long as we're married."

"What won't be in this town?"

He was going to make her spell it out? Maybe even was teasing her some? Getting a little fun out of it? Fine. "Your sex life. Or partners."

He stopped. Right there in the middle of the sidewalk. Then took hold of both of her arms and held her in front of him. So close, if she leaned at all, their thighs would be touching. Glancing up at him, she saw his gaze boring into hers. "There will be no sex life, period," he told her gruffly. "At least not on my part. You think I'd do that to you?"

At that moment she didn't have a thought. Not a single one of them. She had tears welling inside her, though.

And, almost as if he knew the things she couldn't show, knew the battle inside her, Asa leaned in and kissed her.

It was all for appearances, she knew. For the benefit of the folks out and about who'd probably witnessed at least parts of their interaction.

Which was definitely why Lily kissed him back.

She flooded with warmth, too.

Asa was her closest friend. He was going to have her back. Not only during the marriage, but afterward, too.

And that was a win for her future.

* * *

He hadn't thought about sex.

Or rather, entering into six months of total celibacy.

It wasn't a deal breaker. Not even close.

But he should have given the matter thought. Enough to assure Lily that he was not going to be unfaithful to her before she'd had to ask. He would not have her known as a woman whose husband cheated on her during the first year of their marriage. In a town the size of theirs, she'd carry that with her for the rest of her life.

He'd die first.

For that matter, he had no desire whatsoever to be labeled as that guy, either. He planned to be in Chatelaine, owning and running his dude ranch, until he was old and gray. No way he was going to smirch any of it with rumors of infidelity.

Having grown up with all four of the major adults in his life—parents and his aunt and uncle—cheating on their spouses, he'd promised himself he would never put himself in such a situation. One reason he didn't ever intend to marry for real. Or at least not for a very long time.

All of which he'd still been thinking about on Saturday when Lily called him, just after noon, saying she was ready for his truck. With firm wedding plans in place, she'd given notice on her apartment and had been told that, instead of having to pay the full month's utilities, if she was out by the end of the weekend, she'd get her full deposit back. The owner knew of someone else needing a place as soon as possible.

She'd known of someone, too, she'd told him. A cook at work whose twentysomething son was moving back to town to help his father out with their horse breeding business, and she'd hoped the new renter was one and the same.

Asa had wanted to provide boxes and help her pack, but she'd staunchly refused his offer, to the point of refusing to accept his help moving her things from the apartment in town out to the spare bedroom in his cabin, if he didn't stop.

He'd stopped. Asa had figured her sisters would be there, helping her, but was surprised to find her alone. With a tattered blue suitcase, two large moving boxes, and a small closet's worth of hanging clothes wrapped in a blanket and lying over the couch.

"This is it?" He regretted the question as soon as he'd asked it. Making it sound as though her belongings weren't enough.

But in a perfectly satisfied-sounding tone, she told him that the furniture wasn't hers. Her apartment had come furnished.

Standing there, looking at her small, incredibly neat haul, he had to hold back a surge of emotion. He'd been moving around his entire adult life and he had twice as much stuff to lug around with him everywhere he went.

"It's not like I have family photos or childhood mementos," she added. He took the reminder as a cue to get his butt moving.

Carrying her boxes down one at a time, Asa found himself seeing Lily in a new way. It was like he was somehow entering more of her world, even as he moved her into his. He'd known she'd grown up in various foster homes. Nickolas, head bartender at the Corral, and also, as it had turned out, one of Lily's foster brothers, had told him she'd never been in one home long enough to feel a part of a family. Nickolas had only lived with her for part of a year before he'd aged out of the system. But the married man and father of two clearly looked after Lily.

Nickolas was why Lily frequented the Corral, she'd once told Asa. She could have a beer, alone, yet not feel lonely. Plus, she'd help him out in the kitchen, making wings if he got overly busy, and she'd get comped beer.

Asa had known her childhood had been vastly different from his. He'd just never put himself in her position until that Saturday afternoon. Or truly understood how much their marriage was going to impact her life.

And he told himself once again, as they headed out to the Chatelaine Dude Ranch, that he'd make certain his friend never went back to a life of two boxes, an old suitcase, and some hanging clothes.

Unless she wanted to do so.

Wanting to give her plenty of time to unpack, he left her to it and drove to the freeway, following it to the first exit that promised plenty of shopping choices. He wasn't after much. Just a new set of luggage for his bride-to-be, and, as an afterthought, a box of expensive chocolates, too.

She'd raved about a box a customer had left her at the café over the Christmas holiday. He'd thought maybe the drive would open his mind to seeing how out of hand his scheme to get the ranch was getting. Instead, he took the Chatelaine exit feeling pretty damned good about the future.

For him and for Lily.

She deserved so much more than he was giving her, but at least she'd be getting a home, the new way of life she wanted, as she searched for the rest of her future.

The thought was still on top of his mind a couple of hours later, as he and Lily—who'd seemed more embarrassed by, than happy with, his gifts—made their way to the front door of the main house.

Both of them in jeans and short-sleeved shirts, they stood together, their sides touching as they waited for their summons to be answered.

Val looked shocked to see him, but smiled almost immediately as she invited them in.

"That's okay," he said quickly. "We don't want to take up your time, and actually have a lot to do before our flight in the morning. But I just wanted to let you know that I'm getting married."

They hadn't told anyone else of their plans to elope. And weren't planning to tell Val—only that he was going to be out of town and had arranged for Jack to take care of Major for him.

"I heard!" the older woman exclaimed. "But I

thought…" She clamped her mouth shut on whatever she'd thought, and Asa had a feeling he didn't want to know.

He just needed to know that she wasn't going to sell the ranch out from under him while he was gone.

"I've been in love with Asa since last summer," Lily piped in, sounding not at all like the woman he knew. "He'd wanted to make our relationship public, but I…well, I just work at the café and I was afraid people would think I was a Fortune hunter…" Lily looked embarrassed for a second, and then said, "literally," with a chuckle. "But when I heard that you weren't going to sell him the ranch because I was afraid of what people would think of me…I couldn't let that happen. I told him if he wanted to make our relationship known, I was okay with that." She blushed. "Of course, I had no idea he'd do it in such a big way, proposing to me at work like he did, but it's a memory I'm going to cherish forever."

The words rolled so naturally from her lips, Lily had Asa believing them in their entirety. Until he made himself remember what they were doing and why. Maybe Lily had a future onstage…

The absurd thought flew off as Val said, "I heard about that! And the ring. Let me see the ring."

Holding her hand out, and as Val oohed and aahed, Lily talked kind of shyly about being half afraid to wear it, and Asa was fairly certain that she hadn't been faking that one at all. Again, he'd bumbled, doing his thing, solo, as he did. Buying a ring expensive enough for a Fortune, instead of thinking about his bride-to-be and what might have been more suited to her.

He had a lot to learn about being a true friend, apparently. And made it a silent wedding vow to work every day of the next six months to rectify that situation.

He had a ton to do, just getting the ranch ready for the summer season, and was chomping at the bit to get at it…

"I remember your parents," Val said to Lily, stopping Asa's thoughts in their tracks. How did a woman recall one couple from nearly twenty-nine years ago…

"You girls were such a treat that day you were here…in your triplet stroller. They took you to the petting zoo, and I was working there that day, and your parents got you out and you were all just starting to walk. It was absolutely adorable watching you girls toddling around…" The widow hitched in a breath. "And when I heard about the accident the next day I just…" Val teared up.

Lily might have, too. But Asa couldn't see the face she'd turned toward the setting sun.

"We've moved Lily's things into my cabin," he said then, feeling like he needed to rescue his friend. "I'm hoping that's okay with you. I realize I should have cleared it through you first. I just… Lily, as you'd obviously assume knowing the circumstances, couldn't wait to actually live here…"

All true. And would remain true if that was what she wanted. Maybe he'd sell her a cabin on the ranch. Give her lifetime occupancy or something.

Maybe he was getting in over his head.

And couldn't stop the avalanche from rolling forward. Lily had quit her job. Given up her apartment. It was too late to back out now...

"It's fine," Val said, her smile a bit wobbly as moisture still filled her eyes. "Of course she can stay here. I'm honored to have one of the triplets back on the ranch."

Lily still appeared to be admiring the landscape. He heard a sniffle. "What makes more sense than to marry my best friend, who I truly love?" Asa spit out into the moment. All true. Lily *was* his best friend. And he truly loved her. As a friend.

"I married my best friend, too," Val surprised him by saying, drawing Lily's gaze sharply back to the older woman as well. "I wish everyone could. I think it's what made our marriage so strong and healthy for so many decades."

He didn't know about that. Figured, on the inside, behind the family dude ranch scenes, there were some things not as pretty as Val would have them believe. There had to have been some tense times. Fights. That led to...

"And Asa," Val interrupted another pointless train of thought. "You two go get married, and when you return with your marriage certificate and your wedding rings on, I'll have the sales contract ready for you."

Asa found his usual charm long enough to say, "My latest offer still stands." And then, slipping his hand into Lily's, pulled gently, meaning to lead her away. But when she turned instead, looking up into his eyes, he didn't go anywhere. He planted his lips on hers. Right there in front of the widow.

He hadn't meant to kiss Lily. But the way she'd been looking at him, as though he was everything in her world, the light of her life, he'd just bent his head to her lips.

She'd been playacting—for Val's sake. He knew that. But the desire she stirred in him? That couldn't be faked. So much so that Asa pulled back as soon as he felt himself starting to grow hard. There'd be none of that.

Still, as they'd walked back to his place, to share a box of macaroni and cheese and then retreat to their own rooms for a few hours' sleep before needing to get up for the couple of hours' drive to the airport to make their 6:00 a.m. flight, Asa couldn't quite lose the memory of that look in Lily's eyes.

Or the soft touch of her lips beneath his.

Chapter Five

She hadn't ever flown before. However, not wanting to come across as a bumpkin in front of her husband on her wedding day, Lily kept the news to herself. They made it through airport security, followed the signs to their gate, and then before she knew it, they were on the plane. As she buckled herself up, it almost felt as though she'd been doing so all her life.

Finally experiencing something she'd only heard about occupied every single one of her thoughts—and most of her emotions, too—right up until she was sitting there, waiting to take off, anticipating the speed she'd be moving at with a mixture of excitement and trepidation. To distract herself, she thought of her destination.

Vegas.

The strip she'd only seen in movies. The noise

and lights. Millions of people. Maybe, if she'd been heading there alone, she'd have been afraid. As it was, knowing that she'd be experiencing it all with Asa, she couldn't wait.

Wanted to savor every moment.

Didn't want the next two days to ever end.

But at the same time, she didn't want to think about her upcoming wedding. It wasn't that she was getting cold feet. She wanted to marry Asa and had no thoughts of backing out. She just wanted it to be honest and real.

And even though they were marrying under false pretenses, deep down in her heart, her vows would be truthful.

He didn't know that.

His wouldn't be.

She *did* know that.

"Maybe we should write our own vows," she said as the plane taxied down the runway for takeoff. Lily would not reach for him. She couldn't need him *that* much. Instead, she kept her hands in her lap, firmly clutching each other. "That way we can control the lies," she added as they lifted off. "Maybe work our way around them so there aren't so many of them."

Asa's easy agreement was a gift. A distraction.

And got her through takeoff.

They'd said they'd sleep on the flight, since they'd had to get up in the middle of the night to make it to the airport, and Asa drifted off almost immediately. Lily, in her newest pair of jeans and a long-sleeved button-down shirt, closed her eyes, dozed, but couldn't quite get herself to let go and really sleep. Instead, she thought about the one girlie dress she owned, which was probably getting wrinkled in her suitcase, and the shoes she'd worn only once, She'd purchased both for a function she'd gone to with Tabitha's wealthy adopted family shortly after the triplets had reunited.

She'd wanted to get her hair done, but the certificates she'd received were only good at the local shop in the next town over from Chatelaine, and she doubted she had enough money in her checking account to pay for a Vegas hairdo. Like she was some kind of celebrity.

She thought about dipping into her modest savings account for the first time ever, to do just that— get her hair done. And her nails and fingers as well.

If she and Asa ever did get together romantically, as her sisters kept insisting they might, and the day ahead was going to turn out, someday, to be real, she wanted pictorial memories of herself looking... prettier than normal...standing next to her gorgeous cowboy husband.

Plus, people in town, her sisters at the very least, and maybe Asa's too, would want to see photographs from their wedding.

Giving up on sleep, she signed her phone up to the plane's free Wi-Fi and started surfing for hairdos with long straight hair. But eventually settled on beachy waves, not even sure they were still in style, but she figured they'd go best with the kind of longer, rather than round, shape of her face.

She'd need flowers, too. Maybe one in her hair?

The plans seemed to take on a life of their own, and by the time they landed, Lily was too focused on her wedding to pay all that much attention to the crowds, the noise, the sheer cacophony that was the Las Vegas airport and then strip. Slot machines seemed to be everywhere—even along airport walls—as they'd exited the plane with their carry-on suitcases and made their way down the longest escalator she'd ever seen on their search for ground transportation.

Glittering lights and advertisements were everywhere. From the walls of the airport, hanging from the ceiling on the sides of cabs and buses, on billboards…and all of it was like background to her as she thought about standing with Asa and saying, "I do."

But by the time she was in the elevator up to their suite—a feat in itself to reach from the hotel desk—she was overstimulated and ready to escape the crowds.

Yet excited to get back to it, too.

Asa, on the other hand, seemed to take it all in stride. She didn't ask, but figured by the way he knew his way around, that he'd been to Vegas before. He seemed fully focused on getting them where they needed to be, checking them in, arranging the chapel time, and choosing the two dinners, from four choices, that would be brought to their room later as part of their wedding package.

He was kind to her, polite, consulting her on every

decision, and all business. She didn't want to dwell on that.

As soon as she entered their suite, she made a bee-line for the smaller bedroom. Didn't even look at the larger one. Or the view.

Instead, she locked herself in her bathroom, the farthest place from the rest of the suite, and started a three-way video call with her sisters. She couldn't get married, even if it was fake, without letting them know.

After their exclamations of shock over her flying off to Vegas to elope without letting them know, Lily looked from one to the other on the small screen and asked her sisters the question she'd been refusing to ask herself. "You think I'm making a mistake?"

Because even if she was, she wanted to marry Asa. To live with him, regardless of the fact that it was only for six months. To live on the ranch.

And, though it wasn't her reason for marrying Asa, she wanted to be able to at least buy her own home when the six months was through.

"I think you're following your heart," Tabitha said softly, easing some of Lily's stress.

"And who knows," Haley added, "Maybe the marriage will turn real..."

She knew better, and still, that tiny bit of possibility made her tear up—and smile—as she told her sisters she loved them and hung up to their chorus of the same.

She'd told Asa she needed a couple of hours before they got married, but in the end, it didn't take that long at all. He'd told her to charge anything she needed to the room, and, as it turned out, there was a salon right on the premises that offered all of the services she needed, as well as some she didn't recognize.

He might just be closing a deal, making his dream come true, but she was still in the process of reaching for her own dream. And, just in case her marriage to Asa could, by some miracle, turn out to be it, she needed the day to mean more than Asa buying a ranch. Even when it was the Chatelaine Dude Ranch.

He'd suggested that they meet at the suite and ride down to the hotel's on-site chapel together, but she'd demurred, saying she'd meet him at the chapel.

As she'd have done on a real wedding day.

She'd taken her dress and shoes with her down to the salon, not wanting to run into Asa upstairs, and her hour there turned into an impromptu little bridal party with aestheticians gathering around her to take over getting her ready.

It wasn't as good as having her sisters there with her would have been, but Lily actually had a great time, letting herself be pampered for the first time in her life. She exited the place feeling, not exactly like a princess, but more beautiful than she'd have thought she could feel.

The woman who'd done her nails had offered to show her how to get to the chapel, and Lily figured it was kind of like having a bridesmaid there beside her as she arrived outside the room where she'd be making vows that were going to alter the rest of her life.

Then she just plain stopped thinking. She'd waved goodbye to the nail technician, had opened the door to the chapel, and there stood Asa.

Not in the jeans and cowboy boots she'd expected to see on him, but in a full tuxedo. The jacket was black, with silver undertones, and then her eyes drank in the rest of his ensemble. A light gray shirt, tie, shiny black shoes...

If she hadn't already been over-the-top in love with the man, she'd have fallen hard, just at that first sight of him.

He was drop-dead gorgeous.

And in that instant, the small grain of potential possibility lingering inside Lily's chest exploded into full-blown hope.

She let it loose, took ownership.

Telling herself it was just for that one magical day.

What in the hell had she done? Catching his first glimpse of Lily as she walked through the door of the chapel, Asa couldn't breathe.

He'd known she'd brought a dress—they had to in order to keep up appearances. Same reason he'd rented the tuxedo. They'd be getting photos as part of the wedding package.

And people in Chatelaine—Val Hensen, yes, but also his family members for sure—were going to be asking to see them, to share the day.

But... *"Wow,"* he said as Lily walked up to him. He smiled. It was the thing a guy did when a woman got dressed up and walked toward him.

"Too much?" She grimaced, giving him a glimpse of the friend he was going to be spending the next six months of his life with, the friend he loved and trusted, but when she quickly looked away—something she didn't often do with him—he was like a fish out of water again.

"Not at all," he said thickly. "You look…beautiful."

More than he'd ever needed to see. Far more.

The hair, the makeup…she'd been transformed into a bewitching stranger. One his body was responding to in a way that he didn't want to respond to Lily.

The same way it had when he'd kissed her at the GreatStore after their engagement. And at Widow Hensen's front door.

He was not going to go all guy on himself and let sex get in the way. No amount of physical pleasure was worth losing his best friend over.

She still wasn't looking at him. "You want to forget it?" he asked, softly. They still had time to back out. Could walk out that door and call the whole thing off.

Yeah, it would go down as the shortest engagement in Chatelaine history, but that was better than losing Lily, too…

Her face had swung toward him, and her lovely hazel eyes, they seemed to peer so deeply into his that it felt as if she was seeing his innermost thoughts.

"Are you getting cold feet?" Her question had been the last thing on his mind.

"No."

"Neither am I. I want to do this, Asa." Linking her arm through his as their names were called and the inner door to the chapel opened, she confessed, "There's no other man on earth I'd rather marry today…"

Today. He got the disclaimer. Added it to the fact that she didn't even have a boyfriend at the moment, and did that math.

Relieved on so many levels, he was wearing a genuine smile as they approached the pulpit, behind which a character resembling Elvis in a white suit and glasses stood.

Music started. Ended.

The Elvis look-alike, pseudo preacher man—a pretense for their pretense—read a line or two about matrimony, then invited the two of them to face each other, hold hands and say their vows, looking at Asa first.

"Lily Perry, as your husband, I promise you my complete fidelity," he said, the first of the five things he'd come up with on the plane, while trying to fall asleep. "I promise to always have your back. I promise to listen. I promise to keep your needs a priority. I promise to love you for the rest of my life." That last part of the vow was the one he most wanted her to believe. She was his wife for six months, but his friend *forever.* He wasn't in love with her, but what he felt for her was even better. He loved her as a friend. Someone he could argue with, maintain separate though attached lives with, and because he was free to do those things, his love would have no reason to turn into resentment. Or worse.

She hadn't blinked. Or taken her gaze from his. He figured maybe she'd glassed over, was just gliding through the moment that wasn't meant to be real in any way.

"Asa Fortune, I promise to love you for the rest of my life…"

Asa nodded as she repeated his words right back at him. He didn't blame her for not being more prepared with her own set of truth. Hell, he owed her a lifetime of not blaming her in return for the gift she was giving him today.

"I promise to be your wife for as long as you need me in your life." He frowned, looking at her. Not sure where that one had come from. "I promise that you are and will be the only man in my life."

While they were married, he finished the sentence for her. The words she couldn't very well say aloud.

"And I promise to work beside you to make dreams come true."

He smiled at that one. Figuring it to be the best one of all—from either of them.

"Do you, Asa Fortune, take this woman…" Asa held Lily's gaze, trying to let her know that she had nothing to fear and only good to gain as the white-suited man finished his question.

"I do," Asa said.

"And do you, Lily Perry, take this man, Asa Fortune, to be your lawfully wedded husband?"

"I do."

A weight lifted off his chest. He had no idea of its source. Hadn't even realized it had been there.

"Then in the powers vested in me…I now pronounce you husband, and wife. You may kiss the bride."

The smile on Asa's face slipped away. He hadn't anticipated that last line. Hadn't actually given the formal little questions they'd have to answer any thought…

However, the worry in Lily's gaze had him taking a step forward. As a camera flashed, he lowered his head to hers. And understood. She'd been concerned about the photographs. Their proof to the world…

Letting go of some of his tension, he let his mouth open over hers, kissing her as he would any other beautiful woman who was willingly in his arms. Saw flashes behind his closed lids and lengthened the kiss. Because Lily was playing right along with him.

Her arms around his neck pulled his head closer, and he pressed his body against hers…

The next thing he knew, Pretend Elvis was clearing his throat.

Embarrassed, Asa pulled away. He'd gotten a little too caught up in the part they were playing for the camera. And took note.

No enjoying certain aspects of the role he might be called upon to play from time to time.

But figured, as he and Lily went out to the lobby of the chapel and finished up the business of being married, including providing an email to which their wedding photos could be mailed, that there was no reason two friends couldn't celebrate the different, but very coveted futures they'd just locked in for the both of them.

"You want to get a beer?" he asked Lily, dropping her hand as the chapel door closed firmly behind them.

When she said, "Sure," in a perfectly normal Lily tone of voice, he filled up with celebration energy. And it hit him.

Lily had never been to Vegas.

To thank her for being such a sport that day, dressing to the nines to make their marriage appear real, he was going to show his friend the time of her life.

And since they were married, in a deal they both wanted and understood, he didn't have to worry about it seeming like they were on a date.

Watch out Vegas, best friends from Chatelaine Texas, on the loose…

Chapter Six

Lily let herself float on cloud nine during what she considered her wedding reception. She knew it was all make believe, but then everything about Las Vegas perpetuated the sense of an adult fairy-tale land. The lavish resorts that went on for blocks, the opulence, the five-star dining, the oodles of money...

Asa insisted that she try out some slot machines, just for fun. And to her delight, she won, in one push of a button, ten times what he'd given her to spend.

They made their way down the strip, Asa showing her the special features of every resort, like the garden in the five-star hotel where they were staying that was always a different theme, different scene, depending on time of year, but everything was made out of real flowers. The working, full-sized carousel at another place where the entire visible surface was always living plants.

There was the canal through a version of Venice, complete with gondola rides, which they took. Then the fountain that danced to music and an accompanying light display. Another resort was a replica of a New York City street, and the next one—her personal favorite—had a mock Eiffel Tower that they rode up in. Everywhere they went, he had her drop a little into slots.

And every casino they stopped in offered free beer to slot players, too. She could take a bottle with her and walk down the street with it to the next place.

It wasn't a place Lily would ever want to live in, or even visit often, but for that one afternoon and evening, in this stolen moment in time with Asa, her new, *very legal* husband, she was on top of the world. Even after they descended from the tallest tower in the city.

They didn't talk about their pasts, or home. Didn't mention memories or anyone they knew in real life. Didn't talk about families or ranches, dude or otherwise. For those hours, it was just the two of them celebrating in a world of strangers.

Until it was time to head back to their suite for dinner. Asa had called the hotel—twice—to put off heading back, but the ten o'clock final serving time was approaching. They'd snacked on appetizers at one indoor establishment that replicated Greece, complete with full-sized statues, an ornate Parthenon ceiling and painted blue sky overhead.

Still, she was ready to head back. To settle down and eat a full meal. To switch to one glass of champagne along with iced water instead of beer and start to get her feet back under her. To begin to prepare for the vastly changed real life that would be waiting for them when they flew home the following afternoon.

Dinner was served in front of a full wall of windows that overlooked the strip that was as busy at night as it was during the day—with such a glorious array of lights she figured she could just sit and watch all night. And when they were done, and neither of them were quite ready to put an end to the day, Asa suggested they watch the Marvel movie that was being advertised on the nearly theater-sized screen that had been on in their living room when they'd come in.

She'd kicked off her dress shoes the second they'd walked in the door. Had been sad to see Asa shrug out of his tuxedo jacket and vest. And when he asked if she wanted to share the last of the champagne, she nodded, not quite ready to return to real life.

Curling up with her filled glass on the couch, she understood why Asa sat down closer to her than the living room ensemble required. Their seats were directly in front of the screen. And also had access to the table where they could set down their glasses and still reach them.

The movie was good—oddly, the first they'd seen together. He wasn't a talker, for which she was glad. She liked to escape into the films she watched, even when, as was the case that night, she'd seen it several times before.

It was a slow wind down. A bittersweet ending to a fantastical day.

Except that, when the credits were rolling at the end of the movie, she still had a little champagne in her glass and, as tired as she was—having been up since before dawn—she wasn't ready to have the day end. Asa wasn't jumping up, either. Leaning her head back against the couch, she smiled dreamily. "I can't believe we're married."

His lips pursed, then he smiled, too. "I know. Can you believe how much that preacher guy looked like pictures of Elvis?"

"Preacher guy" was the last thing on her mind.

"Your vows were…really nice," she told him, then, turning her head to look at him. "They sounded like wonderful, real wedding vows, and yet, at the same time, fit our situation, too. You didn't lie."

"Nope." He grinned back at her. "You know, even though we aren't lovers and aren't planning to stay married for long, that doesn't mean we don't have a special relationship. Or that we don't care about each other. Personally, I think what we have is a hundred times better."

His words hit her right at her core. Down below and in her heart, too.

She'd have thought going through the fake marriage with Asa would make the love she felt for him seem tarnished. Distant. But as she sat there with him, she realized she was more in love with him than ever. They'd had so much fun together that day, laughing, goofing around, teasing, and yet he'd been completely attentive, too. Had made her feel as special as any real bride would have felt.

His eyes seemed to be speaking to her, holding her gaze for a long time. Until he bent to help himself to one of the chocolate-covered strawberries left over from dinner. She watched unabashedly. Saw the strawberry juice drip out of the corner of his mouth.

And the small piece of chocolate that clung to his upper lip.

Earlier in the day, she'd have teased him about that chocolate. However, this late at night, she was all teased out. "You have chocolate on your lip," she whispered, and reached over to get it for him. Without thinking.

Just doing what she'd do for anyone she loved.

He didn't pull away. Or grin. Instead, his gaze on hers, he leaned forward. Placed a light kiss on her lips. A friend thanking a friend.

Except that she was a wife on her wedding night. One who was so in love with her new husband, she found herself opening her lips, winding her arms around his neck and beckoning him closer... Right or wrong, for this one singular night, in a city where things happened that wouldn't happen anywhere else, he was hers.

And as he deepened the kiss, and his tongue started exploring her mouth, she quit thinking altogether. With inhibitions tempered by the champagne, control lessened by lack of sleep, and a longing desperately eager to be assuaged, instincts she hadn't known she possessed took over.

So when he groaned and pushed gently against her, laying her on her back on the roomy couch, she went willingly. Accommodating his body as he lay halfway on top of her, his thigh between her legs.

She felt air hit her back as the zipper on her dress slid down, and then her breasts were more free to strain against Asa's dress shirt as the back fastener on her bra came loose.

She wanted it all off. Her dress, her bra, his shirt, and when she realized that was his goal, too, she helped him make it happen.

His broad, muscular chest, full of dark hair, was glorious. Her fingers explored every inch of it, before she plastered her palms against him and lowered her head to run her tongue over his nipples.

She didn't know herself. Didn't care.

She'd changed that day. Was never going back to being the Lily Perry she'd been. She had a new legal name. *Lily Fortune*.

And Lily Fortune wanted Asa's pants undone. Her dress came up as his zipper went down, and she opened to him as though there was no other choice. Because for her, there simply wasn't.

He scrambled for his wallet, retrieving a condom. She took the time to stroke him with her hand. And then to help him apply the protection, before she took a deep breath and finally found out what paradise was like.

She'd had sex a time or two. But had never felt such

an instant burst of pleasure. Or actually reached completion simply from a lover moving in and over her.

When it was over, and she was basking in sweet coital bliss, she dreaded going back to reality. So instead, as Asa collapsed against her on the couch, she simply closed her eyes and drifted off.

She was happy. Really happy. For the first time in memory.

Coolness against his backside woke Asa. Or the warmth on his front did. Reaching for covers, he found a naked thigh instead. Not his own. And slowly regained consciousness. Realizing, not only that he was with a woman, but which woman.

Lily?

He'd had sex with *her*?

He had to take it back.

Moving slowly, he extricated himself, but thankfully she didn't wake up as he settled her against the couch. Then, still naked, he went into his room, pulled the sheet and blanket off the bed, and used them to cover his...what?

His best friend. Lily was his best friend.

Wife in name only.

Oh God, what in the hell had he done?

Had he blown everything on the first day? Ruined the one marriage he'd felt good about having before it had even been twenty-four hours old?

Wearing only the jeans he'd worn for travel the day before, he paced his room, figuring he needed to jump in the shower. He glanced out to the living room. Saw the form on the couch.

Pictured, though with the covers, couldn't see, her lovely dress balled up around her waist. He'd taken it off her shoulders, and pushed it up over her hips, but hadn't even taken the time to fully undress her. Of course, neither had she, but...

He'd treated her like some kind of animal.

Acted like one.

And didn't want to risk waking her yet.

Not until he had something to say to her that could somehow save the future.

Lily already thought he was a player. He dated a lot of women. But not because he needed the variety for pleasure. He'd needed it to keep women from wanting more from him than he was willing to give. Things like commitment, exclusivity...

He paced. Ignoring the heart-shaped bed. And couldn't believe he'd been so incredibly thoughtless the night before.

Sex, in an exclusive situation, brought in the strong chance for other kinds of emotions to emerge. Which muddied his and Lily's crystal clear waters. And brought with it the high probability of expectation. Disappointment. Rancor.

He'd lose Lily's friendship. The thought brought on a new surge of anxiety.

He wasn't going to lose her.

But...what if the condom failed and she got pregnant?

Sweating, he thought back several hours to the

moment he'd taken the thing off. Reassuring himself there'd been no failure in the process.

He had to figure out a way to turn back the clock.

To return them to who they'd been the day before, prowling down the Strip, drinking beers, having a great time together. Probably one of the best days off he'd ever had.

This wasn't about saving the ranch—his marriage certificate was signed, sealed, and ready to present to Widow Hensen. It was about safeguarding his friendship with Lily.

She'd follow through on the deal, either way. He was certain of that. But their six months together could get ugly if their hearts became entangled in one another as life mates not just friends.

A future together wouldn't work. Not well. And as soon as they divorced and he started playing the field again...the last thing he wanted was for her to get hurt. And she would if they continued down this path.

"Asa?"

Hearing Lily's voice call sleepily out to him, he didn't answer. Wasn't ready...

"What's going on?" she asked, wiping her eyes as she came to the doorway of the room he'd been frantically walking, as though, if he did his penance, he could be shown the way out the situation he'd created.

He never should have kissed her. Not at the Great-Store, not for Widow Hensen's benefit, and very most definitely not the night before.

He'd been stupid. Surely that didn't have to ruin his entire life.

And Lily's…

Looking over at her, it hit him. "I'm trying to figure out a way to apologize to you," he told her. "I'm beating myself up over breaking my word to you, coming on to you, taking advantage of the moment. I swear to you I've never done anything like that before in my life. And I just need you to know that it won't happen again. Ever."

Her frown didn't bode well.

"But…"

He had to cut her off before she told him she was having second thoughts. "Our arrangement, our marriage, but more importantly, our friendship—which is the one thing that we promised would last forever—is at stake here, Lily, and I can't lose you." If he sounded as though he was begging, maybe that was because he was.

Begging her to let them both forget.

To let go of what they'd done the night before. And to never ever let it happen again.

Because if it did…they were doomed.

Her nod, a knowing look in her eye, told him she got the message.

He stood frozen, awaiting her response.

Was it over before it had fully begun?

"I can't bear the thought of losing you, either, Asa," she said, and turned away from the door.

He wanted to go after her.

Wanted to know if she'd enjoyed their sex as much as he had.

But stopped himself and mustered the control to gather his things and get into the shower instead.

After the initial drop of her heart, leaving a heavy weight in her stomach, Lily walked away from Asa's door just as she'd walked away from every foster home she'd had. Losing one home after the other over the eighteen years of her growing up, never being in one more than a year or two, she knew how to get the job done.

And how to survive.

Asa was just…being Asa. He'd been honest from the beginning about what he did and did not need from her. Or *want* from her.

Just as every foster home had been temporary— by sheer definition of foster as opposed to adopt. And, like Asa, none of the families she'd been with had wanted to hurt her. To the contrary, they'd all been good to her. She liked to think that a couple of them had even loved her.

They'd just had circumstances change, had no longer been able to foster for one reason or another. A husband leaving, a woman being transferred and not allowed to take Lily out of state, an unexpected pregnancy, an illness—the list went on and they'd pretty well all been completely understandable. Even to a young girl craving a family of her own.

It was her silly heart that continued to breed the hope that got her into trouble.

And this time, she wasn't losing her home. To the contrary, she was moving into the place she'd always wanted to live. Temporarily.

But the next time she moved, it would be to her very first home of her own. One she could keep forever if she chose. One no one could ever tell her she had to leave.

And most importantly, this time she wasn't losing family. Because Asa would always be that to her. She'd married him legally. Had taken his name. And they were best friends.

He'd promised to be in her life forever.

A promise no one had ever made to her before.

And...that pesky pinprick of hope that just wouldn't leave her in peace, reminded her, as she packed her bag, that a lot could happen in six months' time.

Men had fallen in love, as opposed to just loving like a friend, in less time than that.

She'd dared to reach out for what she'd wanted, accepting Asa's joking proposal, and look how far she'd come in just a week.

The thought kept her buoyed as she left the suite with Asa.

And on the flight home, too.

Her spirits faltered a little as she rode beside him in the truck back to Chatelaine, to the world where everyone knew her as Lily Perry, the freckled foster kid who was a boy's best friend, not his girlfriend. Who'd grown into a woman who, until the night before, had only ever had sex with a couple of men who'd moved to Chatelaine and then, for various reasons, had left again.

"You've gotten quiet."

It wasn't something he'd have called her on in the past. Friends had their boundaries.

"It was a really busy twenty-four hours. I'm having an energy letdown." She gave him the truth she'd have delivered sitting at The Cellar over a beer. Surface version.

"It seems like there should be some fanfare, you riding back into town as Lily Fortune, married woman." He was grinning.

Looking sexy as hell.

His ring glistened as the sun shone through the windshield, and she looked at the matching white gold band on her own hand.

And it hit her. In that moment, she *was* a married woman.

In every sense of the word.

The realization put a smile on her face, too.

Chapter Seven

The second he pulled onto the long drive leading onto the Chatelaine Dude Ranch, Asa was hit with a need to get busy. First and foremost, visit Major, let the boy know he was back and still the same old Asa.

And to check on the rest of the horses, too, most of which were used by patrons of the ranch. They'd been his responsibility since moving to town. Something he'd offered to do for Val Hensen when she'd agreed to take him on as a permanent border in one of the family cabins that had always only been used as vacation rentals.

Dropping Lily off at the cabin, he purposely left her alone, giving her time to move about the space alone, to get her bearings and handle any phone calls she might want to make in private.

He knew she'd been living alone a long time, and

he wanted her to have the time and space to do whatever it was she did at home.

And maybe he was running away for a few hours. Just to find his own bearings. Getting back into his routine would help him put everything—the old and the new—into healthy perspective. Then all he had to do was keep it there.

A quiet ride on Major helped solidify the calm his mind had finally found.

And just as quickly, any sense of peace he'd found flew the coop as he rounded the lane toward his cabin and saw Val Hensen's golf cart at the front door.

He'd been planning to visit the widow in the morning, with a check in hand.

Pulling the truck into his usual spot beneath the trees at the side of the cabin, he jumped down and tried to look as casual as he could as he hurried inside.

Lily was sitting on the couch with Val, and Asa stopped just inside the door of what had been his bachelor pad until a day ago.

He'd had a lot of different living quarters over the years, but hadn't shared them with anyone since he'd left home at eighteen.

Even before then, he'd had his own room. A place where, when the door was shut, no one was permitted entrance without him there.

Lily glanced at him. "I've just been showing Mrs. Hensen…"

"Val, please," the widow interrupted. "I told you, please call me Val, Lily. We're going to be family now with you and Asa adopting my husband and mine's firstborn, the ranch…"

"I've just been showing Val our wedding photos," Lily said then, turning her phone so he could see the current shot. Of him in his tux, standing in the gondola, holding a hand up to help her down.

Val reached for her purse and pulled out a thick envelope. "I brought the contract for you to sign," she said, her tone changing to all business. "Lily's already shown me the wedding license…"

She unfolded several long pages, joined at the top, and moved to the wooden table that served as both eating spot and desk to him. He joined her there.

Skimming the contract he'd already seen when he'd first submitted an offer to buy the ranch months before, he took the pen she offered and signed his name.

It took all he had not to let out a huge whoop and holler as he handed the pen back to her. The moment was solemn for the widow. No matter how badly she was in over her head and wanted to be able to travel to stay with her kids for longer periods of time, signing away a lifetime had to be incredibly difficult.

"And now you." He heard Val's words. Saw her hold out the pen in Lily's direction.

What was going on?

Had the two of them…

"Me?" Lily asked, and Asa grew warm with shame. Thinking for one second that Lily would have gone behind his back, made some deal with the widow…but…

"I'm selling to a *family*," Val explained. "Asa knows that. Come on, sweetie, it's your new life, too..." When Lily looked at Asa, not standing to join them, Val said, "Unless you don't really want the ranch. If this is just Asa's choice and you..."

"No!" Lily jumped up. "You of all people know what the Chatelaine Dude Ranch means to me," she said, moving slowly toward the table. She didn't even look at Asa as she took the pen and signed her name, just beneath his. On a line that read *spouse*.

That's when reality hit Asa. The whole of what he'd done. Letting Lily do him a favor. Knowing he'd return the gift in kind. It wasn't anything as simple as that. They'd gotten the law involved when they'd run off to Vegas.

And while he didn't doubt for one second that Lily would sign the ranch over to him when it came time to dissolve the marriage, he no longer felt like whooping and hollering.

At all.

Instead, invisible bands of truth and desperation, of subterfuge and shame, wrapped around him. Trapping him right where he'd sworn he'd never be.

In a relationship from which he couldn't just walk away when unhappiness took root.

She couldn't stop shaking. Inside, and a little bit outwardly, too. Hugging her arms, Lily sat and listened as Val explained the workings of the ranch, much of which Asa already knew so she didn't go into all that much detail. She turned over a key to the office, talked about bookings that were going to be arriving over the next few weeks—even in February—and said that she'd been packing for weeks and had arranged over the weekend to have movers there the next day.

Lily heard her, took it all in on some level. Mostly she just heard her head repeating the same words over and over. *I'm part owner of the Chatelaine Dude Ranch!*

It meant nothing. She knew that. No way she'd hold that signature over Asa's head when it came time for them to divorce. She valued their relationship, and her own integrity, far more than any piece of land. No matter how precious to her. Or how lucrative.

And, still...

I'm part owner of the Chatelaine Dude Ranch?

For twenty-nine years, her life had been predictably unremarkable. The biggest event had been moving from one home, one bedroom, to another. Having to learn a new address and foster parent phone number.

But in the course of a week, she'd gotten married to the man she'd been besotted with for months, had had hot, passionate sex with him, had quit her job, moved to the land she held most dear... And now owned half of it.

She could be forgiven for having a case of the jitters. And a moment or two of surreal mental aberrations.

Val was thanking them, holding out a hand, which Lily took, and then walking out the door. When that wooden structure closed behind the widow, Lily would be alone with Asa, in the two-bedroom cabin meant to be a vacation rental for families.

A cabin that they both now owned.

There was so much to think about, to learn, reins they would need to take up immediately. The ranch had a handful of employees, people who'd be doing their jobs during the transition, keeping things running smoothly, all folks who'd been working with Asa over the past months.

While Lily, the new owner for a few months, blathered silently about none of it.

"Feel like getting a beer?" Asa's question, the normalcy of it, reached out to her like a lifeline.

The Corral. *Their* place.

"Sure." She grabbed her keys and then dropped them in her purse. She wouldn't need to drive separately.

They'd be leaving from and returning to the same place.

Not at all normal.

Downright weird, really.

Especially when one considered the twelve-pack of his favorite brew she'd seen in the cabin's refrigerator.

He seemed to be losing Lily. Couldn't figure her out.

The Corral had seemed a logical solution. Not only because they'd met there, but because the majority of their friendship hours had been spent there.

Just running into each other and hanging out.

But as soon as they walked in together Monday, wedding rings on their fingers, the place erupted into clapping, and then, as they sat, they were besieged by a series of visits to their table from well-wishers.

It took an hour for them to finally get some peace.

At which time he said, "You okay?"

"Yeah."

"It doesn't seem that way." *Don't talk about sex. Please don't talk about sex.* He didn't want to hurt her. Or to want her again, either.

Head lowered, she looked up at him. "It's all so strange. I can't find anything that feels like me." She looked around them. "Even this place, tonight."

"Yeah, but look, it's already settling down in here. The rest will, too."

She nodded and sipped the one beer she'd been nursing since they came in. "The signature means nothing," she said then. "I have no intention of taking half of your dream. Or forcing you to change the plan."

"I know." But it felt good to hear her say it. Did that make him scum of the earth? "All that stuff Val was saying tonight, about duties she's expecting you to take over…you don't have to do any of it." She'd said when she'd first accepted his facetious proposal that she'd been planning to ask him if she could help out at the ranch once he owned it. But that was just so she could spend time on the property.

She was frowning. "What else would I do?"

"Take the time to figure out what you want to do for the rest of your life. Take some classes if you want." Granted, opportunities were limited in a town the size of Chatelaine. And she'd told him many times that she had no desire to leave the town, ever.

It had come up when she'd mentioned some guy she'd dated briefly. He'd moved to town as part of a team doing road improvements for the state and had asked her to leave with him, to see if they could make a relationship work.

"I want to work at the ranch." She'd raised her head, signaled for another beer, and was looking him straight in the eye. "Everything Val said…the list of events coming up, bookings, the growing wedding venue side of things, the little café that's open during the summer months—that's a given for me—I want to do it, Asa."

Her eyes had the old light in them. Pre-engagement. Something he most certainly hadn't seen since she'd appeared in his doorway in Vegas that morning.

"Then you shall," he told her, finding himself more relaxed, and strangely more excited, too.

"Okay." She grabbed a small notepad out of her purse, pulled the little attached pen out of the elastic at the side, and started writing as she spoke. "I handle guest relations, planning and arranging events, administrative and staff management duties where it pertains to any of that, and you handle everything ranch related. The petting zoo, farm animals, obviously the horse and horseback riding as you're already doing, tours of the property and wooded trails, maintenance staff, and whatever else you envision. How does that sound?"

Better than he'd thought it might. Good, actually. "Fine," he told her, nodding.

"Then sign here." She passed the small notepad over to him.

He read the brief agreement she'd drawn up, then looked over the list. Added, *and anything else that comes up*, to his part of it, and signed, passing it back to her for countersignature.

There was no touching. Not even a finger brush. Nothing at all that could be considered "more than friends."

Merely two people getting on with the rest of their lives.

Just as they'd planned.

That night after they got home, Lily called the bathroom first, and then retreated to her room, closing the door firmly behind her. And on Tuesday, they both hit the ground running so fast there wasn't time to think about marriage and sex—or even to dwell on basic matters of the heart like being head over heels in love with a man who only saw you as a friend.

She and Asa kept in contact over radios, both listening to the channel active for the small staff, and then talking to each other on a private channel Asa had set up for them.

All business.

She was the new face of the Chatelaine Dude Ranch to the public, and to the staff. The learning curve was huge. But she found herself catching on, knowing what to do, without a whole lot of guidance. Val was there on Tuesday, showing her everything. The widow, who'd bought a small place in town, had said she'd be available by phone whenever Lily needed her and offered to come out to the ranch to help out in the office if she was needed.

Lily hoped not to have to make that call.

Gaining confidence by the second—she'd always been an excellent student—she'd mastered the on-line booking system, the basic filing system, and the banking all before noon.

With a full afternoon ahead of her.

The one personal conversation she had with Asa that day was borne from her new confidence. Bol-stered by the fact that she'd dared to reach for more, for her heart's desire, and had found a life she hadn't even imagined for herself.

A temporary one, for sure, but once she'd gotten the hang of going after what she wanted, rather than settling and finding her happiness with what she had, who knew what lay ahead.

She called Asa on his phone, midafternoon, from the bare kitchen in the main house, not on the radio.

"Lily? Is everything okay?"

"Great," she told him. "Though we're going to need to make a run to Corpus Christi to buy kitchen supplies. And furniture. My pot and pan, and your little toaster oven aren't going to fill even one cup-board of this place. And all the empty rooms…"

"Fine. You can start by ordering whatever you want that'll ship, and we'll set up a time for furniture shopping. I'll open an account for you at the bank as soon as I've finished out here with the cows. I'm hoping to start some basic rodeo activities to offer guests by summer..."

She listened as he talked about adding calf roping and a controlled cattle drive, then went on to talk about skeet shooting, but didn't let herself get distracted from her purpose.

"Asa? I have a request. Not quite a condition, as it's a bit too late for that, but it's important."

"What?"

"Dinner. I want us to eat dinner together at night."

Silence met her on the other end of the line.

She'd been prepared for it.

"First off, it's what families do, what I've missed my whole life. And since this is supposed to be the start of my dream come true, as well, and my request doesn't change the boundaries we set forth, I feel that it's a fair ask. Second, it'll be a set time each day we can discuss ranch business. After just one full morning at it, I can see where we're going to be too busy to see each other much, and we'll need some quiet time to discuss things."

"Request granted." His response didn't lag even a second. And she smiled.

Pictured him smiling too on his end.

She and Asa really were best friends. They knew each other, understood each other.

And if that was the most she ever got from the man, she'd be happier than she'd been before she'd known him.

More content than she'd ever been.

And there came a point when allowing yourself to be happy with what you had was just plain smart.

Chapter Eight

Asa didn't care a whole lot about the furniture he used. He needed it to be there when he needed it. And to comfort tired muscles as necessary.

Realizing that if they didn't get to Corpus Christi—the nearest town with enough shopping choices—and get some furniture in the house, they'd have to spend another night cooped up in what had turned out to be a far too small cabin, he'd taken off at midafternoon on Tuesday, emptied out the back of his truck, and picked up Lily.

He'd even managed to have the forethought to call her first and obtain her consent to the plan.

The hour-long drive to Corpus Christi had been consumed with ranch talk. And they hadn't even covered a quarter of what he wanted to discuss with her. So far, they'd just been getting started with current and pending business. He had ideas he wanted to run by her. A slew of them.

But first, "Seriously Lily, pick what you want. What you think the house needs." They'd found a huge furniture store, divided by types of rooms and were still just in the living room portion. They had both a living and a family room in the house. One had a wall of windows with screens that looked out over the ranch. The other had a fireplace.

"It's your house, Asa. Tell me what you like. Or, if its easier, what you *don't* like."

He didn't like having to choose. And told her so. "I trust your judgment. Everything you've had me sit on was fine, other than that gray sofa set we both disliked. Besides, it's your house, too, at the moment. And when you move to a place of your own, you're going to need furniture there. It's only fair that you get half of whatever we have together."

The thought had only occurred to him as he said the words, but when he saw the surprise, and then warmth spread over Lily's expression, he knew he'd come through. Not just for her, but for himself, too.

She was helping him build his dream future, and he would do the same for her. Not when their marriage was through, but from day one, just like she was doing for him.

That's what you did when you loved someone.

Even as a friend.

Furniture purchased, at least the start of it—with the two bed frames, headboards, footboards, and mattresses loaded in his truck, and the rest, including a third bedroom set for the guest room, living room set and kitchen table, on schedule for delivery to the ranch on Wednesday—Asa suggested dinner out.

It wasn't a date. Not even close. Just the dinner they'd agree to have together each night to discuss business.

He just hadn't been prepared for the first order of business that came up. She'd taken charge of the meeting from the time they'd been shown their booth in the Mexican restaurant they'd both wanted to try.

"I need to know something," she said, holding his gaze when he'd been about to peruse the menu. He was hungry. She had to be, too.

"What?" he asked, hoping it was about the different types of jalapeños the waitress had described as she'd seated them.

"Would you be willing, assuming that I do a good job, to keep me on in my duties at the ranch once our marriage agreement ends?"

Not a food question. Or one that he'd been at all prepared to be hit with.

"It's not a deal-breaker, Asa," she said, her tone carrying no disappointment with him. "It's a practical consideration, really," she continued, putting her napkin in her lap. "There are a couple of weddings on the calendar, including your sister's, by the way, but I'm guessing you knew that. In any case, one is for fall. And then there are the bookings, and café menus, which I'd like to change according to season. But if I'm going to jump in and start all of this, but not be there to finish—most particularly with the weddings—I feel as though I should alert customers to that fact. We can just say I'm only working temporarily until we can find someone to handle the management duties..."

One of the things that had first drawn him to Lily was her ability to see through minutia and focus on matters at hand. The first night he'd met her, there'd been a run on wings at the bar and she'd slid off her stool, washed her hands, put on gloves, and cooked up more wings.

All that *after* she'd already put in a twelve-hour day at work and would need to be back for the early shift in the morning.

Then there'd been that night where there was talk in the bar of family trouble with someone everyone knew, serious trouble, and Lily had sat there on her stool, chatting with him, sorting out emotion from fact as though the problem were her own. She'd homed in on what she'd figured was the real problem—jealousy—and she'd turned out to be right, too.

"My personnel problems aren't yours to worry about," he started in, seeing her leap into action to problem solve for him because that was just Lily's way. He was absolutely not going to take advantage of her.

However, he knew the second the words left his mouth, they'd been the wrong ones. "That didn't come out right," he said then.

"No." She didn't let him get anything else out.

Opened her menu. "You're absolutely right," she told him in that tone that had always seemed normal to him, but suddenly sounded distant. "I don't think I'm going to try the jalapeño tasting plate…"

With one finger, he pushed her menu down so that he could see her face.

And she could see his.

"Lily… I feel like a real jerk here, getting everything I want while you… I just don't want to take advantage."

There. He'd said it. And then more came. "What I need to know is if you want to work for the ranch… past our agreement. But how could you possibly know that if you haven't done the work yet? What if you hate the job?"

"I guess then it would be like any other. I'd put in my notice. Whether we were still married or not."

She wouldn't. Not while they were married, at least. He knew her well enough to put his life on that one. But six months wasn't all that long to do something you hated.

If it turned out she hated it.

"I wasn't kidding when I said I'd already been planning to ask you if I could work at the ranch before the whole marriage thing came up," she said then. "I was just thinking about maybe helping out at the little café or something…"

"Just because you wanted to be on the property regularly." He reiterated what she'd told him. He'd paid attention.

"Right, but also because I didn't even think about

being able to actually quit my job and do a lot more. I loved every minute of what I was doing today," she told him then, her eyes glowing as they had a time or two in Las Vegas. "My head is spinning with plans, changes I can make to have things run more efficiently, like the seasonal menus at the café, and maybe a cotton candy machine in the summer, and caramel apples in the fall…"

She took a breath and then said, "I'm applying for the job, Asa. Right here. Right now. I'd like to know if it's available and if I'm a likely candidate. Before I invest too much of myself into it."

Wow. He smiled. He couldn't help it. He'd wanted her to bloom, rather than just accept what was in front of her, and she was sprouting petals all over the place.

With flecks of gold, he thought, taking in the freckles that set her apart from any other women he'd ever dated.

"The job is available. And you're hired," he told her. And he could not, absolutely would not, touch her again. He'd rather die than be the cause of her wilting. "With the caveat that if you find that you don't like it, or want to do something else, you let me know. Whether we're still married at the time or not."

She smiled. "Deal," she told him, and gave her attention back to her menu.

Leaving Asa to wonder how on earth he'd turned out to be such a lucky guy.

Lily hadn't known it was possible for her to be so happy. Other people were the blessed ones. Not her.

She'd have figured they'd be tired, arriving back at the ranch after nine o'clock Tuesday night. Had expected they'd spend one more night in the cabin, and unload their beds in the morning. But Asa cracked open a couple of bottles of beer, handed one to her, and told her to pick her bedroom.

She chose the one at the back of the upstairs hallway, right next to the bathroom, and with a view of the ranch. Leaving the master, with it's bath included, for him.

It made the most sense, since he was the one who'd be living there long-term.

It didn't take him long to get her bed set up. When she'd said she was going to take the four-wheeler back to the cabin to gather sheets and a bag of things for the night—towels, toiletries, clothes for the morning, pajamas—he'd opted to go with her, to get his own.

The entire way there, and part of the way back, he'd talked to her about plans for the ranch. Wondering what she thought of adding rodeo-like activities for guests, and maybe allow local kids who had an interest in rodeo to come out to work in the same corral, for real, when guests weren't using it.

She'd told him she'd call their insurance company in the morning, to see what kind of coverage the activities would need, and work up a cost estimate for him.

It was all businesslike.

And yet...invigorating, too. Two weeks ago, she'd never in a million years have pictured her and Asa riding in a four-wheeler across the Chatelaine Dude Ranch together, ever. Let alone at night.

"You want to take a detour and drive by the rest of the guest cabins?" he asked her. The housing units were all in the same general area on the ranch, six arranged in a semicircle around an outdoor swimming pool and playground equipment and four others, Asa's being one of them, set off alone for more privacy.

"Of course." She sipped from the beer he'd opened for her, not caring that it was getting a little warm, and felt the cool, sixtyish degrees night air against cheeks suddenly warmer as his arm brushed hers.

Who cared about making beds or getting some sleep? She felt alive, really alive, and didn't want to miss a second of the joy by sleeping it away.

The thought was fanciful, she knew it even as it came to her.

And she thought of her sisters, figuring they'd be proud of her, as she sat there thinking about putting her hand on Asa's thigh.

He'd said no more sex.

But he'd wanted her. She might not have had a bevy of lovers as he had, or had much experience at all, but she'd felt his urgency even before he'd entered her.

And had taken that ride right along with him, too, ecstasy and all.

She'd talked to both Haley and Tabitha when she'd returned from Vegas the day before, and again that morning, too. Keeping them updated on what was going on. She hadn't told them she'd slept with Asa, though.

That was private.

During the course of their conversation, she'd invited them to come out and take a walk around the ranch with her. To come out anytime they liked, in fact.

While the ranch was her home, she wanted them to consider it theirs, too. To share the place with them, as the three of them had shared it with their parents on their last day on earth.

She'd like to think her parents were happy for her.

"Esme called today," she said then, naming his younger sister, who was also her friend. "Since she wants to have her wedding here, at the ranch, I told her to come over tomorrow and we'd get started on the planning..." She was rambling. Filled with so many emotions that had no business spilling all over him. "But...before I actually speak to her, I need to know a couple of things."

"Name them." If only she could be a little more like him, taking everything on the chin instead of in the heart.

"First, I need to know what you told your sisters. About us."

"Same thing everyone else knows. We're married."

"And they believed that? Knowing you? And me? They really think we're in love and married for real?"

His shrug didn't give her much. Except more desire to be as calm as he was.

He glanced at her as he said, "You're the only woman I hang out with on a regular basis, and have ever since moving to town. It made perfect sense to them."

Which meant she was going to have to play the loving new wife to her new husband's sister—her friend. And…it was what she'd signed on for. But it didn't mean it would be easy.

"You said a couple of things." Asa nudged her with his elbow. "What's the second?"

"Everyone's asking me…are we going to have some kind of reception? People want to party with us. Personally, I'd much rather not, but I know Esme's going to press me about it tomorrow and…" She glanced at him. "I think if we want everyone to buy into us together—and most particularly Val Hensen—then we need to do something…"

"So let's have a party. And if you're willing to take them on, I'll leave the details up to you."

As if life was just that simple. But she agreed. Because to not do so would bring on a conversation she wasn't prepared to have.

Asa had slowed their pace as they approached occupied cabins and he talked about updates he'd like to make to them. Painting. Some new cabinets and fixtures. He mentioned that he'd been hoping to put an indoor pool in, as well, but with the higher price he'd paid for the ranch, figured that might have to wait a year or two.

And she smiled, then, thinking that, as of that night, she could count on still being on the ranch then.

As long as she didn't put her hand on Asa's thigh.

He was accommodating all of her needs and wants, and she had to give him the same. He'd made it clear that he didn't want a real marriage.

She couldn't push that.

Another sobering thought struck her then. What if his excitement on their wedding night, his desire, had been a product of Vegas, of alcohol, of him imagining he was making love with any of the sexy women they'd seen on the strip that day. What if...

She stopped the thought.

Wouldn't disgrace herself, or the memory of those moments with Asa in their honeymoon suite by entertaining what-ifs.

And yet, a small voice reminded her, she wasn't Asa's type. He'd been honest with her about not wanting sex with her.

"What's wrong?" He'd stopped the four-wheeler in front of a currently vacant cabin with occupied ones on either side of it.

"Nothing, why?"

"You just tensed up," he said.

"It was just a chill."

His brown gaze was compelling as it focused on her beneath the security lights shining around the pool in the distance. "You sure?"

She met his gaze. Held it. Valuing his friendship and all that they were doing together far more than mere sex. "Yep," she told him and took another sip of beer.

The look in his eye, the raised brow, the shake

of his head, all left her knowing that he wasn't convinced. But he didn't call her on her lapse, either.

When you were just friends, there were some things you didn't share. Besides sex.

"Just friends" had boundaries that didn't allow some of the heart-wrenching honesties shared by husbands and wives.

And, finishing her brew, she said, "You ready to head back? We need to get those beds made and get some rest. We both have long days of work ahead of us tomorrow."

He gave her one last long look, and she hoped, for a second there, that he'd refuse to head back just yet. That he'd push her for more.

Instead, he nodded, put the four-wheeler into gear, and shot them at top speed back into the life they'd agreed to share.

Chapter Nine

For a second, Lily thought about doing her hair, dabbing on a little bit of the makeup the salon had sold her in Las Vegas, for Esme's visit the next morning.

She was supposed to look different, right? The glowing bride?

In the end, she pulled on jeans and a long-sleeved button-down white shirt, slipped into her only pair of cowboy boots—purchased for a country dance at some point—and ran a brush through her hair. Leaving it hanging long.

Because, yay, she no longer had to pull it back, or pin it in a bun, for work at the café.

And made a mental note to do some online shopping for a few more shirts. Her entire adult life, she'd spent more hours in her uniform than anything else, and her closet contents didn't support even a week's worth of different outfits for ranch work.

Esme had been new to town just before the holidays, showing up nine months pregnant with her baby boy to be with family after a hard marriage that ended when her husband died. Poor woman had then found out that her three-month-old baby had been switched at birth and wasn't hers after all. Good news was, she'd ended up with two baby boys, instead of one, and a loving man as a bonus. Lily had heard the saga every step of the way as it was happening, in stereo. Asa's version as he retold parts of it to her at the Corral. And Esme's version, too, as the younger woman and Lily had hit it off the first time Esme had stopped at the café, a bit harried, as her newborn had decided to wake and let her know he was unhappy right when she'd been in the middle of shopping. Lily had let her use the break room to feed her little guy in peace.

The fact that Asa and Esme had turned out to be brother and sister had been like an omen to Lily. What it had been predicting, she didn't know, but she'd been glad to be friends with both of them. They were orphaned, too, though as adults, and in Lily's world, that had kind of given them a special bond.

One that mattered to her a great deal.

Which made her nervous when she heard the ranch's reception door open a little before ten on Wednesday. Her office, in the back across the hall from the coin-operated laundry room available to guests, was blocked from view of reception and the check-in counter, but she could see via security camera who'd come in.

And went out to greet her friend.

She was surprised by the big hug Esme gave her, but returned it in kind.

And then realized that the affection was based on them being new sisters. Only, she knew they'd only be such for a few short months.

The pang that accompanied her as she led Esme back to her office seemed to be growing inside her, in spite of the joys that were also abundant in her new life.

She didn't lie to her friends.

And, other than her sisters, she was duping the entire town that had been her only family since she was ten months old.

"Where are the boys?" she immediately asked, as she noticed her friend without either of the four-month-olds she was raising.

"Ryder has them. Just until I get back," Esme said, her creamy skin creased into a smile that lit the room. The lovely brunette had most definitely lost the shadows that had clouded her green eyes the first few months Lily had known her.

But as she smiled at her friend, she felt a prick of envy, too.

Which was absolutely *not* her. Jealousy served no good purpose and opened the door for bitterness to grow.

Something a foster mother had told her along the way. She couldn't remember which one. She'd been pretty young. The words had been offered lovingly, not in a mean way. And they'd stuck.

Esme deserved every single good thing that had come to her.

And maybe Lily reaching for more wasn't such a good thing after all. There she was, with more than she'd ever dreamed of having in her lifetime, and she wanted more? Wanted Asa to love her like Ryder loved Esme?

Wanted to have babies with him?

Shaking the thoughts right out of her head, she sat down with Esme, conscious of her VP fiancée's family merger and acquisition business responsibilities, and her friend's need to get back to her babies.

She pulled out a snapshot book of previous weddings held at the ranch, intending to show them to Esme, but her friend shook her head. "Uh-uh. Not yet. First, tell me when and where you and Asa are having your wedding reception? Because you have to have one, Lily. If anyone deserves to have the whole town showering her with gifts, it's you."

Asa had left it all up to her. Kind of a deflating thought. Who wanted a party for two that only one cared about?

"Well…"

"Good," Esme said, with a nod. "Bea was going to call you, but I told her I'd talk to you about the party when I saw you today. I already called Haley and Tabitha, and they are on board with the idea…so if it's okay with you, we'd love to throw you and Asa a wedding reception. We were thinking at the LC Club."

The same place Asa had wanted to take her and her sisters the night they'd gotten engaged.

And she still didn't want her first visit to the place to be a fake celebration. He'd left all the details of a celebration up to her. Clearly hadn't had interest enough even to make suggestions.

"I really appreciate this…but would it bother you all too much if it was held at the Corral?"

She saw the surprise cross Esme's face. And continued, pushing forward when, in any days past, she would have simply nodded and gone along with what was being offered. "It's where Asa and I met. Where…we…fell in love. And maybe more people could come, you know…"

Because not everyone had a lot of money. Some of her friends from the café, for instance. And Nickolas, with his wife and family…they did fine, but no way she'd want them to fork out money for a babysitter, plus gas out to the LC Club, and then…even the drinks there were twice the cost of the Corral. She'd looked online once.

"No, that's great!" Esme said, all grins as she sat forward. "I love it! And my brother will probably thank the heck out of you…"

They talked about dates. Esme wanted to wait a couple of weeks, because if they did it too soon, more people would be booked up, and then, when Lily started to make a suggestion or two, perhaps catering in some food from the café being one of them, Esme shook her head. "No way, girl. This one's being done *for* you. Not *by* you."

Not used to being the center of attention, Lily nodded.

She wanted to tell Esme to let everyone know not to bring gifts. But had a feeling that even if she did so, she'd be ignored on that one.

And if her marriage to Asa was real? Would she still say no gifts?

She wouldn't.

But who wanted a bunch of reminders of a broken heart? Which was what she was likely going to be left with when the union ended.

Turning the wedding book around and shoving it across the desk right in front of Esme, she turned the talk to a real wedding. One conceived in love.

Asa, on the four-wheeler, was heading back from the horse barn, when he saw his sister's vehicle parked outside the reception area. He was about to head up and say hello to her when he heard voices hollering.

"Jimmy! Jimmy!!" The first voice was male. The second female, and ending on a scream.

Making a sharp turn, he headed down the road toward the cabins and met up with the distraught couple on the way. Stopping, he got the gist in a couple of seconds.

Their four-year-old son was missing. They'd been walking the family path in the woods with him and their three-year-old. The little one had fallen and both parents had turned to him. When they turned back, Jimmy was gone.

The younger boy, Willie, was riding on his father's hip, and still sniffling.

On his radio immediately, Asa alerted all staff that a four-year-old blond boy named Jimmy was missing and for everyone who could to report to the family trail immediately.

He heard from Lily before he'd even signed off. On his cell. She was on her way down. Esme was helping to search up nearer the office in case he'd headed up for some candy or something.

Telling Lily to arrange the search party of the woods, Asa left the parents and took off on the four-wheeler. He'd seen the little guy the day before, by the fishing pond not far from the cabin area. If he'd wondered off...

The pond wasn't all that big. An acre, maybe. Man-made and fed, too. But for a young child...

If the boy had only been missing a few minutes, even if he'd fallen in, there was still time to save him if he didn't waste a second. None of the three families on-site that week had signed up to fish that day. Chances of anyone being at the pond to help the kid were nil.

He took the four-wheeler as far as he could. About thirty seconds up the road, and then took off on foot. The boy, even running, wouldn't have been at the pond long. He would only have had five minutes on Asa at most.

Ripping through trees, his boots clomping through brush, Asa broke into the clearing near the pond and nearly wept.

Jimmy was sitting on the ground, a kitten in his lap.

Out of air, Asa slowed his step, calmed his breath, so as not to scare the boy, and walked slowly toward him.

"What have you got there, buddy?" he asked, while he was still far enough away for Jimmy not to feel immediately cornered. The boy was right on the edge of the water. Asa didn't want to scare him into falling in.

"A baby cat," the boy said, looking over at him, his voice still more baby-like than Asa would have expected. "You're the man with the horses." The *r*'s were rounded.

Asa smiled. "That's right." He pulled out his radio. Quietly announced his location and that he had Jimmy in sight as he approached the boy.

Jimmy seemed more interested in the kitten shoving its head into the boy's palm than the man coming toward him. "There's a cat at the horse barn," the boy said, rubbing a hand on the kitten's head.

Kneeling down close to the boy, Asa murmured, "There's more than one of them." Wild cats that hung around. The Hensen's had allowed them to breed to help keep mice and other rodents under control.

Asa and Lily hadn't yet gotten anywhere near as far as discussing the presence of the cats. Or what to do with them.

"Maybe this is one of her babies. I had to rescue him so he didn't get too lost…"

"Maybe it is. If you come with me, to my cart, we can get you back to your Mom and Dad, and then I'll take the kitten to the barn," Asa offered.

"Okay, but only if you promise to take care of him," the boy said. Standing, and with the kitten hanging over his arm, he lifted his other hand toward Asa, as though expecting them to hold hands for the way back.

Taking that little hand in his own, Asa felt a clutch at his heart. Picturing his four-month-old nephews... thinking of them at Jimmy's age. Or Willy's. Running all over the ranch...

And for the first time, thought about, maybe someday, having a son of his own. He didn't see how that would happen, didn't want to muck up another life as his parents had mucked up him and his sisters.

But in a perfect world...it might be cool to have a little guy around all the time. To help him grow into a man.

The thought wasn't even complete before Lily showed up on the four-wheeler he'd given her to use as her own, Jimmy's parents and little brother aboard.

And where Jimmy might have received a scolding— after the frantic hugs from both of his parents—Lily intervened. Jimmy had told his parents why he'd run off, and both of them had started in on him about how dangerous that had been and not minding his rules. Lily interrupted, suggesting that they all drive the kitten to the horse barn together, returning it to his parents, just like Asa had returned Jimmy to his. Pointing out that as scared as Jimmy was for that little kitten, wanting to get it home, his own parents had been even more scared about him.

Speechless, Asa sat there, staring at her.

Had the woman just taught the boy a lesson he wasn't likely to forget? Without a single harsh word?

Asa had no way of knowing, of course, as they all drove off to the horse barn, leaving him alone at the pond. He even told himself he was overreaching.

That the whole marriage thing, finally owning his ranch, was kicking him a bit off-kilter. He'd be more himself in another day or two. Once he settled into the routine that had driven his entire adult life.

Then, returning to the matter at hand, he got on the radio to thank everyone for their quick responses and rode off to the cow pasture.

Where the manure he got himself into washed right off.

Since word of Jimmy's having been found had been sent over the radio to those searching up by the store, Lily had expected Esme to be gone by the time she was heading back to her office. They'd already outlined the basics of the wedding before the 911 radio alert had come through. She should have known Asa's sister—the new mother of two baby boys—wouldn't leave until she heard all the details.

She picked up Esme in the four-wheeler when she spotted her friend walking along the road she'd sped down half and hour before. Immediately, Lily relayed the news of Jimmy not having so much as a scratch on him.

"What a relief!" Esme exclaimed. "I stayed on the road the whole time. I figured, if anyone came this way with him, I'd see them," the young mother told her as she climbed in.

Lily shuddered at the chilling possibility that had been clearly weighing on Esme's mind. That Jimmy had been kidnapped by someone who'd looked decent enough to get onto the property, but who was rotten on the inside.

Reminding Lily of the other woman's not so distant rough past. With a man who'd promised to love and cherish her, but who'd broken her heart instead.

Lily wanted to hug Esme. And had an aha moment, too. An hour ago, she'd been envious of her friend. But when she looked at her own life…she'd only ever been treated with decency.

And that was something for which to be deeply thankful.

For which to feel lucky, even.

She filled Esme in on the kitten details. And then said, "Another good ending, just like with your boys. Them being switched at birth was just accidental, not some sinister plot."

"Absolutely," Esme said, then added, "I still wonder about that mysterious volunteer who was there that night, but knowing that the nursing assistant realized she put the wrong bracelets on the babies…it's always good to have faith in humanity reaffirmed."

"Always," Lily concurred with a nod. "Asa's the one who found Jimmy, by the way."

"I'm not surprised," his sister said, smiling.

Pushing the gas pedal, Lily turned and headed back toward the office as Esme confided, "You have no idea how thankful I am that you hung in there with him."

Hung in there? Frowning, Lily shook her head. "I don't get it."

"Asa's a master at blowing off the women in his life. He does it kindly, of course. From the very beginning. Letting them know that he's not boyfriend material, or open to any kind of ties or exclusivity, as I'm sure you know. He'd have done it with you, too. But you didn't let him push you away."

They'd reached the office. Lily needed to escape inside. To put her mind to the hundreds of tasks awaiting her. The myriad of things to learn.

Not sit and be reminded of unrequited love.

Or dwell on having to lie to the woman with whom she'd developed a real bond within a short period of time. A woman she'd love to call sister for real.

Another random foster mother quote came to mind. Something about tangled webs you weave when you deceive.

"He...didn't push me away," she said slowly. Thankful that she could speak the truth, in this matter at least. "But I never acted like I expected anything from him, either," she added. "Because I didn't." All factual.

Which felt better than any alternatives she'd come up with. Like saying out loud that what made her different from all the rest was that Asa had fallen in love with her. She just couldn't give voice to the lie.

"Maybe that's what did it," Esme said then, her

tone growing even softer. "Women have always been all over him."

"I noticed." Lily's dry comment just slipped out. Accompanied by an eye roll.

Esme patted her hand, still on the steering wheel—as though she could drive away from the entire conversation. "Like you have anything to worry about," she said then. "You're the only one who's ever snagged him."

She found that a little hard to believe. In his adult life, yeah, but when he was younger... "Even in high school?" she asked, and then felt like she'd been unfaithful to Asa by doing so. Going behind his back for information on his life was so not her way of doing things.

"Especially in high school," Esme said. "He had his eye firmly on the door, not on finding any reason to hang around." Esme's sigh carried a lot of lived-life in it for one so young. "I don't know how much he's told you about our growing up, but it wasn't pretty. Or kind. Our parents fought. A lot. They had affairs on each other. I found books. Fairy tales, and later love stories. Feel-goods. When there was fighting in the house, I'd take my books and escape into the woods with them."

"That must have been very difficult for you as a child," Lily said quietly.

"Yeah, it was, but the upside is that even though I grew up with unloving parents, I still believed in love. Couldn't wait to grow up and fall in love and have a family. Which—" she shrugged "—maybe made me a little too eager to find it the first time." Esme shook her head and then continued. "Asa, on the other hand, stayed there, like he had to make sure no one got hurt or something. To make it worse, our aunt and uncle were the same way, unfaithful to each other. Always fighting. And it left him, I feared, unable to believe that romantic love even exists. Until you."

Tearing up, the younger woman touched Lily's hand again, squeezing it. "I'm just so thankful he has you." She sniffed. And then straightened. "And now, before I make a total fool of myself…I'm off to rescue my fiancée from our sons…"

With a smile, she was gone.

And Lily, who had so very many things to do, sat in the drivers' seat, going nowhere at all.

Chapter Ten

Asa worked like a madman the rest of that week. Taking care of the horses, as he'd already been doing, getting a corral ready, with bleachers just outside it to accommodate the new family rodeo activities he wanted up and running by summer. He worked with the two young men Val had hired full-time to help with the running of the ranch, promoting them both, which basically meant giving them more responsibilities, putting one in charge of updating the petting zoo, new paint, fixing boards in stalls and fences, and the other in charge of the new corral. Even though Val had already hired a local man to come in and mow once a week, Asa knew they needed more regular help, so he went ahead and hired a recent high school graduate, a young man who'd grown up in foster care, to work at the ranch full-time as their landscaper.

He also called a pool guy to refinish the pool and to fix the heating system.

In the meantime, Asa put himself in charge of setting up horse riding lessons for the local kids who didn't live on ranches, and put both of his cowboys on schedule to teach them.

And he spent time on Major, re-riding every inch of the ranch, taking notes and pictures. And just taking time to let it all in. To believe he'd actually made it.

What he didn't do was leave time to run into Lily. They were in touch on their private radio channel all day long. And he kept his word to her—met her at the house for dinner every night. Sometimes fixed by him, if she was still in the office, other times, prepared by her and he'd come in when it was ready. They discussed ranch business while they ate. And then he made it a point to keep himself busy outside the home until he saw her bedroom light come on upstairs.

It wasn't right. Wouldn't last long-term. He knew that. But for that first week, it got him through.

He missed breakfast with his sisters on Saturday. They tried to get together every week, but he couldn't get himself to make it happen, using his newly acquired ranch as an excuse. There was just no way he was ready to sit alone with them, or with Lily, and have them picking at his marriage.

They'd do it lovingly of course. But he wasn't ready to have them looking too closely.

Not after he'd gone and had sex with his best friend.

He'd been finding himself noticing her at odd times throughout the week. Seeing her on the four-wheeler, leading a new family to the cabins on Friday, for instance.

Not one damned thing sexy about that.

But his mind had gone straight to Lily's gorgeous body moving temptingly beneath his on that couch in Las Vegas.

He just needed time. Distance from the wedding day.

So much was happening so fast. Monumental life changes. As it turned out, realizing his dream after twelve years of backbreaking work was a lot to process.

So it made total sense that he'd feel some backlash.

Lily had detailed some of his sister's wedding plans for him over their nightly dinners. Discussing the somewhat luxurious lodge that the Hensen's had used for all kinds of events, from barn dances to wakes to weddings. Lily wanted to repurpose a barn that had once housed the Hensen's small, personal beef cattle operation into the event center, take out a part of the back wall of the lodge, making it floor-to-ceiling windows overlooking the woods filled with hiking trails, and adding an outdoor gazebo with cleared ground for seating for the actual weddings to take place when weather permitted.

She was hoping to have some of the work completed in time for Esme's wedding the following month.

He'd seen his sister's vehicle on the property a couple of times. Had smiled each time. Couldn't be happier for her.

And felt a major prick in his sense of well-being when she texted him on Saturday, asking him to meet her and Lily at the lodge—a rustic, though quite nice place, complete with ballroom area for holding events.

The fact that she'd sent the request, not Lily, made him uneasy.

His business partner had conceded the task for a reason. He didn't like not knowing what it was.

As if Lily and Esme were in cahoots. Concocting something he might not otherwise go for.

And, perhaps, he was letting his conscience get the better of him—pretending to be in love, and married for life—and needed to just suck it up and quit overreacting to everyday things.

It was just… Esme, with her soft heart and quiet intelligence, tended to see through him more than most. Which could prove to be a major problem for obvious reasons.

"If the gazebo isn't ready, we could do the ceremony here," Lily was saying as he walked in through a back, service door. "With the right lighting, maybe strings of little white lights, it'll make the place look more magical. I can set this area off with white lattice room dividers, white wooden chairs for the guests, and the aisle would come from there." She pointed to a hallway leading to the restrooms and a back area currently being used for storage. "I'll have that room cleared out, carpeted, with changing areas, couches, mirrors...make it into a bridal suite...and then the reception can be in the ballroom area."

Her words broke off as she and Esme noticed him.

He was smiling. Couldn't help it. Lily was the best.

Whether she was serving coffee or planning dream weddings, she gave everything to the moment.

"Don't let me interrupt," he told them.

Esme grabbed his arm, pulling him toward the potential wedding area. "You aren't interrupting," she responded, dropping his arm. "Ryder and I want a simple, traditional wedding," she said then. "We're each picking out a couple of our favorite passages from books to read as part of the ceremony. Lily and Bea are my bridesmaids..."

He looked at his friend at that one. She hadn't mentioned that she'd been asked to be in his sister's wedding. She'd need money for the dress and...

They hadn't had a single personal conversation in days. He hadn't even asked how she was doing.

"...and Ryder's brother Brandon and Linc Mahoney are the groomsmen."

He'd been left out. Disappointing, but best that he not be paired with Lily, walking her down the aisle.

"The two couples will each be walking a stroller down the aisle with the boys in them," Esme was continuing. Painting a picture for him. One that made him happy for her. "That part was Lily's idea, because I wanted them included somehow..."

Asa looked over at the woman he'd married the week before. Wondering if it was hard for her, planning a real wedding when hers had been...not that. Knowing she'd never let it show.

He wanted to tell her that she'd get her chance. As soon as they were divorced and she embarked on her new life, in a real home of her own, she'd meet someone, fall in love...

The idea didn't make him feel all that much better. More conscience backwash, he was sure.

Her attention all on Esme, Lily didn't even glance his way.

"And then the next part is where you come in," Esme was saying, yanking Asa's gaze straight to her. His sister grabbed his hand and pulled him a step closer. "I'm hoping you'll walk me down the aisle, Asa. That you'll give me away."

Him? In a tux again so soon? Walking down a wedding aisle? Esme deserved someone who believed in that stuff.

But... "Of course I will," he told her. And as she teared up, he didn't nudge her as he would have done any other time. Or lighten the moment with teasing. Instead, his chest tightened and he pulled his little sister into his arms. Silently promising her that he'd give her away, but not completely. Not ever completely. He'd be having her back until the day he died.

It wasn't until he'd pulled back that he realized Lily had walked away.

She was inspecting the back storage area. Giving him and Esme their private family moment. As a friend would do.

Funny, how it bothered him so much, her always ending up alone like that.

If anyone deserved to be included in close family moments, it was Lily.

Not him.

Esme had been gone about an hour on Saturday, when Asa stopped by the office.

"This place looks great," he said, looking around from just inside the door. It was the first time he'd been to her new space since their first day of ownership.

Lily had rearranged furniture so she had a picturesque view of the property from her desk. She had also thrown out two grocery bags of things that were of no use to her and Asa, and had been through the entire filing system. Fortunately, Val Hensen had kept great records, and had them in easy to follow order.

"It's getting there," she told him with a happy sigh. "Now that I know I'm going to be working here long term, I'm thinking I'd like to paint the walls—they're so smudged and dirty—but that can wait a good while." Business. It was all they talked anymore.

"You want to go get some beers?"

He wanted to go to the Corral? Had he read her mind? Did he know how badly she missed his friendship? "Now?"

His shrug was off, not easy and casual like before. "Maybe after dinner."

"Okay." She glanced over at him, still bothered by the somber look on his face. "Or we could go now and have wings for dinner."

It was the Corral. It *wouldn't* be a date.

And dinnertime was for business talk, so if that was what he needed, if he had something to discuss with her that he wasn't sure she'd like, best do it at the Corral.

Where her feelings would be under wraps, as though held by the people in town who, collectively, were her family. In the house she was currently sharing with Asa, she felt too raw.

Made no sense, but there it was.

He offered to drive. She accepted. No way she could see him riding around in her little beater. And it would be too weird for them to drive separately. In the past it had made sense. They'd been coming from and returning to two separate places.

So much change, so many nuances, she hadn't considered.

She led the way into the bar, waving at people as she went, heading for the only open table, in a back corner of the front room. She and Asa usually sat at the bar. But for some reason, she didn't want to eat up there that night.

He didn't say anything about her change in seating location. Just dropped into the chair across from her and pulled the wing menu out of the metal holder at the end of the table. He suggested a combo platter.

She agreed, and, rather than waiting for table service, he went up to the bar to place their order. Came back carrying two beers.

She took hers. Sipped. Telling herself to relax, as she faced another first.

The first time she was nervous sitting at the Corral with Asa. They'd promised to be friends forever, but it was beginning to seem like, after only one week of marriage, they were hardly friends at all.

His gaze almost accusing he asked, "Why didn't you tell me that Esme asked you to be in her wedding?"

Whatever she'd expected to come her way, that was *not* it. She frowned, not at all sure where he was going with the question. "Because she didn't want anyone to know she'd chosen her bridal party until she asked you to walk her down the aisle."

"Why not?"

"I have no idea." She told him the truth. "I didn't ask." Then added, "But I can take a guess if you want me to."

A muscle ticked in his jaw. "Please."

"She didn't want to make the announcement without you in it."

His features relaxed for a second. But not long. And she waited. They might not be acting as friends, or in any way normal around each other, but she'd known him, adored him, for a lot of months, and could still at least read his expressions with some accuracy.

"You haven't spent any of the money I deposited into an account for you."

Again, not anything she'd expected him to be bothering about. Him going crazy having her living in the same house as him...*that* wouldn't surprise her. But this threw her for a loop.

"I haven't needed to," she told him. "I've been working full-time since I graduated high school, and it's just me. I've got a little bit of money put away."

"And?" he asked when she stopped talking, keeping the rest to herself. Maybe she wasn't the only one who could read faces.

"And I don't like it that you can see the account, see what money goes out and where." There. She'd said it. "If we were really married and had a joint account, then I'd be fine with it, but it makes me feel like I'm your charity case, or kept woman or something, you having ownership on my bank account. Or even depositing into it like that. I'd rather just get paid from the ranch like everyone else."

He watched her. She could see his features softening, almost like he was morphing back into the man she knew right before her eyes. "Or, for the time we're married, we could have a joint account, with all profits from the ranch that aren't going back into the business, deposited into it, and we both spend from it personally as needed."

Her heart leaped. He wanted a joint bank account? You didn't do that if you were only into something for a few months.

"And when we split, we'll divide whatever money is in the account equally. Then the ranch can start to pay you."

Or maybe you *did* do it even if you were only in it for a few months.

Remembering her sister telling her to hold on to hope that the marriage could become real, Lily nodded. And felt like she'd been thrust over rapids and come out intact on the other side. She nodded as Asa told her he'd take care of it on Monday, as though they'd been discussing…fat veins in beef. Something he'd have talked to her about in the olden days.

So hard to believe that had only been a week and a half ago.

Putting his beer down after a long sip, he said, "This is all really strange, huh?"

"Yeah. Kinda." Completely, one hundred percent.

He signaled for another beer. Took a long sip after it arrived, and said thickly, "I feel like I'm losing you."

Her heart leaped up and started to thud. Hard. "You aren't going to lose me," she assured him, able to pour herself fully into that response. "If you haven't figured it out by now, I value your friendship more than just about any other."

Or, maybe more than any other, period. Her gaze dropped to her beer. From the night she'd met Asa, something in her had settled. As though she'd met her soulmate.

Which was why she was in the predicament she was in—tangled up in truth and pretense. Because Asa had needed her, so she'd needed to be there for him.

His finger touched the back of her hand, briefly. Enough to get her to look up at him.

"You know that I consider you my best friend, right?" he asked.

She'd thought so. *Hoped* so. Then nodded, more tentatively than she'd have liked.

"The sex is the problem," he blurted then. Softly. But it hit her like a megaphone to her ear. "It's like there…between us…holding us apart."

Was he saying he wanted more of it? That wanting it was what was in between them?

"We can't go back and undo it," he continued.

"Do you want to?"

"Hell, yes." His head dip emphasized the words even more critically. To the point that her mouth dropped open in horror.

Apparently her expression was so filled with shock, she didn't even notice until Asa said, "Oh, hell, Lil, that didn't come out right." Reaching over, he took her hand. "I'm not saying it wasn't great. Because it was. But that's the crux of the problem, right? If it hadn't been good, we'd both have shrugged it off, and it wouldn't still be here mucking things up between us."

She'd never, in a million years, have considered their lovemaking to be something negative, but with what Esme had told her the other day about Asa, about them growing up, and him living his whole life ensuring that he was never ensnared as his parents had been, she understood what he was saying.

Enough to lose some of the anguish his *Oh hell* had immediately stirred within her.

"It's not mucking things up for me," she told him

then. Thinking of him. And of herself, too. "We're healthy adults, Asa. We'd had a bit to drink. Things happen sometimes. Like…sometimes, when there's white cake around with buttercream frosting… sometimes I just eat too much of it. It's there, tempting, and I'm free to help myself to it, right? So sometimes I do. That's all."

Not quite. By a long shot. But, sort of.

"White cake, huh?" he asked, a slow grin spreading across his face.

She shrugged. "Only with buttercream icing. None of that whipped crap for me." She grinned back. Just as she'd have done any other time they'd been sharing beers together.

He nodded. "White cake," he said again.

"This is what I missed this week," she told him then. Something inside of her pushing to be heard. "This right here. You and me."

His face sobering, he nodded again. Looking her in the eye. "Me, too."

And she wasn't quite done. She could roll with most punches. Could take all the change happening overnight. She just didn't want lose him. She'd bear it if she did. She'd find her happiness wherever she ended up. A lifetime of doing so told her that.

But she couldn't just sit back and take it this time. She had to fight for him. "It seems to me that people quit being friends when they quit sharing…whatever it is they share," she told him. "This…" She pointed between the two of them, their beers, their conversation. "This is what we share."

"And right there is why you're my best friend," he told her, grabbing her hand again, giving it a squeeze. Sending her insides into a major quiver.

Giving her hope.

And then letting go.

Chapter Eleven

Saturday's conversation with Lily at the Corral stayed with Asa as he dived into ranch business the following day. They'd stayed for hours, drinking and then sobering before he drove home. Discussing ranch business a lot of the time, but only because they were both so invigorated by the task they'd taken on together.

Their chitchat the night before was what prompted him to stop by the office for her when a call came in about a water leak in the cabin they'd just rented the day before. A young professional couple looking for a few days away from work was staying here. "Since you're the one who checked them in, I thought maybe you'd want to do your thing with them, make sure there's nothing else that's not to their liking, while I fix the sink."

"You thought maybe I'd entertain them while you fix the sink," Lily said, grinning as she followed him out to his four-wheeler. "You're definitely a guy who likes to be left alone when he's on a project." She stuck out her tongue as she finished.

And his groin grew instantly.

At the sight of that teasing, moist, tongue.

What the hell…

However, his immediate problem disappeared as quickly as it had arisen when he pulled up to the cabin to the sound of tense voices coming from an opened window.

Lily glanced at him. "Maybe there's more than just a water leak? You sure that's all they said was wrong?"

The couple had called the ranch's maintenance number, which rang to a cell phone Asa was carrying until he could hire a full-time maintenance man. Mr. Hensen had handled a good bit of the ranch's fix-it problems himself during his lifetime, but after he died Val had called a guy in town anytime she'd had a problem.

"That's all they said," he told her, grabbing the plumbing bag he'd put together when he'd sorted through tools earlier in the week.

Tense sounds came again, male that time. He couldn't make out the words.

"Maybe we should come back," Lily said, but he shook his head.

"I told them I was on my way."

She didn't have to accompany him. He was still

glad she did, though, as he climbed the couple of steps to the cabin's front door.

He'd barely ducked under the kitchen sink before he quickly diagnosed the problem—a crack in the trap—and went to shut off the water, pulling a new trap piece out of his bag as he returned to the kitchen. Grabbed his little can of purple PVC pipe glue, too. And the pliers he'd need to unscrew the old trap and apply the new.

Then heard Angela Larson, one of the cabin's two guests, say, "I think maybe we're going to check out early." Clearly addressing Lily.

He stopped forward motion just as he was about to slide back under the sink. Stood up. And saw Brad Larson, standing in the middle of the living area, hands in his pants, looking at his wife as though she'd sprouted some kind of body part he didn't recognize.

Looking as bewildered as Asa had felt the night before.

"Because of the leak?" he asked inanely, when he had no business doing anything but fixing a leak and letting Lily refund part of the couple's payment to the Chatelaine Dude Ranch.

"No," Angela said, looking at her husband, before turning her gaze to the two of them. "Because once we got here, we figured out that there was nothing we wanted to do."

"I want to fish," Brad said, as though needing to point out the lie in his wife's statement.

"I want to horseback ride," Angela shot back.

Lily shook her head, frowning. "We offer both of those activities here."

"Yeah, but the whole point of this trip was to do things *together*." Angela again. She looked from Lily, to Asa, who'd started to sweat a bit, then toward her husband, and finally back to Lily. All the while Asa's head was ordering him to vacate, telling him he should have listened to Lily and retreated, rather than putting himself in the vicinity of a marital battle.

He'd had enough of that growing up. Always thinking he needed to stick around so none of the people he loved—including the parents who didn't seem to love each other—got hurt. Or did something irreparably stupid.

"We've...kind of...grown apart," Angela admitted then, addressing Lily specifically. "I'm a lawyer, he's in finance. We both love our jobs. And..."

"You hardly talk to each other anymore?" Lily asked, glancing at Asa, who stood there, watching her.

And then heard himself say, "My wife can tell you, I learned, not too long ago, that the way to find your way back to each other after a...separation... is to talk to each other. Not as husbands and wives, but as the friends you were before you got married."

He was speaking to Angela. Sort of. Mostly, his gaze kept straying back to Lily.

Realizing in that moment that their conversation the night before had been far more momentous than he'd realized. He and Lily would make it through their temporary marriage, intact, as long as they continued to be friends throughout the process.

He could do that.

And, of course, he'd have to stay off the white cake for the duration. No matter how tempting the buttercream icing might be in the moment.

"Do you like to hike?" Lily asked then.

"Yeah." Both of their guests said at once.

"So maybe you quit trying so hard and head out to one of the trails. We've got all skill levels. Getting back to nature, away from the world, exercising, working off tension, doing something you both love…might be good for you," she said.

That was his Lily. Always able to get to the meat of the point and toss out the minutia that smothered so many chances of reaching an understanding.

"And talk," Asa blurted, feeling like, as the host, he should be a part of the solution, too. "Just talk like you used to. Even if it's about work."

He'd had a great time the night before, better than he had all week, discussing business with Lily. Once they'd figured out how to be "them" again.

"I'm guessing there's still good feeling between you both, or you wouldn't be here," Lily's soft words hit Asa strongly.

Good feeling.

Yeah. That's what he felt when he hung out with Lily.

Angela glanced at Brad, who was looking right back at her. "There's definitely still some of that," he said tenderly.

At which point Asa dived for the sink. Sliding himself into the cupboard and attacking the plastic.

He didn't need to witness any of the mushy husband-and-wife-making-up stuff.

He and Lily definitely wouldn't be needing that.

Lily spent the rest of the day Sunday buzzing inside with replays of her and Asa that morning with the Larsons. She and Asa…marriage counseling? It was ludicrous. And it fit, too. Asa wouldn't live in a rancorous marriage. He'd fix it, or kindly end it, taking the brunt of all burden in doing so upon himself. He wasn't a guy who hung around in unhealthy situations.

Asa just didn't seem to see that about himself.

The Larsons had walked up to reception together, later, to thank Lily, asking her to pass their thanks onto Asa, too, for caring enough to share a little bit of marriage advice with the two of them.

Apparently it was all they'd needed, a middleman to help them see through the job tensions and distractions to find their way back to each other.

They'd scheduled horseback riding for the following day. And had rented fishing poles, too. Two of them.

Asa came in to make dinner with her that night—a first, them in the kitchen together—and she told him about the visit from Angela and Brad.

"I guess we got it right, because being best friends kind of is at the core of having a successful marriage," she said, brushing against him as she reached for the colander hanging from a decorative holder she'd put on the wall—her breast touching his chin for a second—while she was talking. He stopped peeling the cucumber he'd had in hand. Just stood there at the sink, saying nothing.

Minutes later, as she'd poured hot pasta into the colander resting in the opposite side of the sink, she caught him looking at her breasts.

And tingled all over.

He looked away.

She did as well.

And they both tried to pretend it hadn't happened.

Over dinner, they talked ranch business, as always, and the moment with the colander seemed as though it hadn't been.

Which put Lily into another quandary. Had his reaction just been an involuntary male reaction to his skin against a breast? Because a ladies' man had locked himself into six months of celibacy? Or... just because he was a guy who couldn't help it that he liked breasts?

Or had it been an *Asa* to *Lily* thing?

She liked broad shoulders. But Asa's shoulders were the only ones she'd ever been so wildly turned on by in the throes of passion, as they were moving above her, that they drove her over the edge. And, even now, drinking in his big, strong presence made her ache to go to bed with him all over again...

She swallowed hard. But she doubted he felt the same way about her. She was very much aware that, with her freckles, her stick-straight hair, and her lack of sex appeal...she'd never been anywhere near the smoking hot category that Asa fell into.

Still, when he asked her if she wanted to sit out on the porch and have a beer before turning in, she couldn't help remembering that electric moment between them at the sink.

Wondering if…just maybe…it had had something to do with his invitation.

She sat on the porch swing. Asa took a big wooden chair bowed at the back as if made to fit a human spine. They talked about Esme's wedding some.

Asa mentioned that Jimmy and his parents and little brother had stopped by the barn that day, before they left, to visit with the kitten. He'd ended up giving it to them.

"You what?" she asked, stopping the swing to stare at him. "That's really cool, Asa! And you're only just now telling me?"

He shrugged. "It's just a kitten."

"Maybe. Or perhaps, to that family, it'll be just a kitten like Major is just a horse."

His glance up at her was probing. Like he was looking for more than was there. Reminding her of their wedding night.

And she got hot. Inside. And so very wet.

Couldn't stop staring at his mouth. Remembering…

Until she almost fell off the swing. And stood instead. Her nearly empty beer bottle in hand, she made to move past him. "I…um…think I'll turn in," she stammered. "We've got two check-ins in the morning, and I want to double-check the cabins to make sure they're ready, plus I've got another three weddings on the books—all from out of towners—and have to get working on the lodge if I hope to have a decent bridal suite in time…"

She was rambling.

Trying not to look at his mouth again.

And ended up with her gaze on his crotch instead. Outlined in those sexy, tight jeans.

Completely visible by the light through the living room window in front of which he sat.

Of course, she tripped. Because of the bulge. The sight of it had taken every ounce of her focus. Then, to her dismay, the toe of her slipper, caught the inside of his boot, right at the arch, and she would have fallen, if he hadn't caught her.

In one arm, due to the beer bottle in his other hand.

Laughing, embarrassed and jittery, she quickly righted herself.

Or tried to.

Asa's hand that had steadied her, caught hers. Yanking her down to his lap, and before she could figure it all out, his lips were on hers.

Devouring her.

Then his hands found her breasts and she arched against him.

Opening her legs, she straddled him in the big chair. Riding his very obvious desire through their two pairs of jeans, and still getting herself off.

Right before she exploded, Asa stood, holding her in place against him with one arm, as her legs wrapped tightly around him.

He made it inside the front door. To the couch. Kissed her again as his fingers worked her fly. He stripped down her jeans, undid his own fly, and was inside her, riding her as she bucked, until they both came to full pleasure at the same time.

Euphoria had never been so all-encompassing. So intense.

Or so fleeting.

Lily knew, the second she came down, that while Asa had most definitely found physical pleasure, he was not sharing her joy.

He'd stiffened almost immediately. Pulled slowly out of her. And then had jumped up off the couch as though he'd been burned.

Closing his fly and fastening his belt, leaving his shirt hanging over it, he was still breathing a little heavy as he said, "I'm sorry."

She'd been a little slower at gathering herself. Was only just getting her jeans up over her hips when she heard the words.

And had no idea what to do with them. Was he apologizing to her? Or just sorry in general that he'd done what he'd done. Did it matter?

"Me, too," she told him. Because at that moment, after what they'd shared, to hear him say he was sorry about it…she wished it hadn't happened, either.

How did a woman feel good about her future, her chances at happiness, when the man she loved with her whole heart regretted making love to her?

"Look, I don't know why this is happening, but it can't mean anything, Lil. And we can't keep doing it."

The distress in his tone was so clear, so painful, she knew that for both their sakes, she just had to accept the truth.

Not fight it.

"I know," she said, heading across the room toward the stairs. She stopped with one foot on the bottom step. "But just so *you* know, Asa, I enjoyed it."

Chapter Twelve

I enjoyed it.

What in the hell was the woman trying to do to him? With one hand she'd fully accepted that sex would not be a part of their lives. Had never once tried to convince him otherwise. Yet with the other hand, she tempts him?

To be fair, she hadn't done a thing to bring on sex that night. She'd tripped over his big, booted foot.

He'd done the rest.

With her cooperation, yes, but no surprise there. He knew how to please women. He'd had a lot of experience.

And she hadn't.

No way the woman was teasing him.

To the contrary, she'd been nothing but the friend she'd been since the first night they'd met. Sincere. Loyal. Accommodating. Asking for…so little.

Too little.

Which was why it had felt great to give her so much. A way out of the dead-end life she'd been living. Fulfilling her heart's desire with a home of her own. A permanent job at the ranch for as long as she wanted it.

He was the one who was blowing it.

She hadn't changed. Not even in the clothes she wore. With decent money at her disposal she hadn't splurged on designer clothes. Wasn't wearing makeup or having her hair and nails done.

So why was he suddenly so attracted to her?

Because the question just brought sexy visions of Lily to mind—visions he absolutely could not entertain—Asa pushed the wondering away and did what he always did when faced with a problem. He moved through it, over it, or around it.

Except…without knowing why…how did he define the problem? Sex was the result. But what was the problem?

And then it hit him.

On their wedding night, when they'd had sex, the look on Lily's face, the abundance of happiness in her gaze…he'd felt like a million bucks, being the guy that gave that to her.

So…maybe it wasn't about the sex. It was about making Lily happy. Maybe it was *that* look he was craving.

Satisfied that his deductions had a great chance of being accurate, Asa hooked his horse trailer up to his truck, left the ranch before dawn Monday morning, and headed out of town to a ranch he'd once worked for. They were nationally renowned for breeding some of the best quarter horses in the States. A family business, they'd been breeding horses known for their temperament and longevity for more than twenty years.

He'd thought about calling first, to make certain that he'd find what he was after, but decided just to show up. And pour on the charm and even resort to past relations, if he had to, to make sure that he left with a gorgeous young mare.

One that had been earmarked to keep for breeding.

"I'm not going to breed her," he told Mark, one of the brother owners, and the man who'd offered Asa the top management position to get him to stay on. "I'll sign paperwork saying so. I'm not trying to compete with you. I just want the best of the best for…my wife."

Why the words came out Asa had no idea. He hadn't been planning to spread word of his marriage any further than Chatelaine. Partially because then he'd pretty quickly have to spread news of the divorce, too.

But Mark had to know how vitally important this gift was to him. Why the quality mattered.

"No way, man! You're *married*?" Mark glanced at Asa's left hand. Saw the ring there, grabbed his hand and shook it. And then kept shaking his head all the way to the barn. "I can't believe it! Asa Fortune has gotten himself hitched! There must be broken hearts all the way across Texas…"

Asa took the ribbing in stride. He'd earned it.

And would be back to earning it again at some point.

He also paid for, loaded up, and took home his first-choice pick. A two-year-old dam—old for breeder weaning, but the average age at which the bond between foal and mother naturally ended.

A gorgeous, shiny brownish red, the girl was a beauty. He couldn't wait to get her back to the ranch. Played with various scenarios as the miles passed behind him. He'd pull up to the office, have Lily come out to the trailer. Let her lead her girl down into her new life.

Or…maybe he'd get the dam set in her stall in the barn—the one right next to Major—and decorate a little. Make it more like a wrapped present. And let her and the girl bond there in privacy.

He thought about saddling her up, asking Lily to go riding with him, and when he and Major and Lily and the girl were out on the ranch, telling her that the dam was hers.

He'd texted to let her know he'd be gone for the morning, had even told her he was visiting the ranch he'd worked on prior to moving to Chatelaine. To see the owner.

Because they were business partners and he'd be leaving her alone on the ranch.

Because he hadn't wanted her to need him and not be able to find him.

Because he wouldn't be on the ranch radio if any problems arose.

Like a missing kid.

The thought reminded Asa of the little guy reaching for his hand that day at the pond. And him having an out-of-body moment where he'd thought he might want a kid of his own someday.

What had *that* been about?

His mental question went unanswered as another flash occurred to him. The previous night. On the couch.

He hadn't used a condom.

He'd hit the call button on his steering wheel before the period planted on the end of that sentence. Told the automated system who to call.

"Asa? Are you back?" Lily sounded as though she'd been involved in something when she picked up the phone. Like she wasn't giving him her full attention.

"No, not yet."

"Is everything okay?" she asked worriedly. "You sound—"

"We didn't use a condom," he blurted. There were things she could do. Take a morning-after pill. He'd had a woman tell him about it once when she'd asked him not to use a rubber because she didn't think it felt as good.

He'd opted out of sex that night, instead.

"I'm protected, Asa. I take contraception for... female regulation."

Something he most definitely should have known about his wife. Even in name only. He tried to hold himself in check, to remain completely calm and serious as the relief flooding through him made him slightly giddy.

"Was there anything else?" Lily's voice came over the phone.

And a vision of her—pregnant—came to mind. Not a horrible sight.

She'd be radiant.

Wearing a Mona Lisa smile.

She'd be the best mother ever, too.

He just wasn't going to be the father.

"No," he told her.

And hung up.

Lily wasn't at the ranch when Asa returned. His phone call, the obvious horror that had prompted the call, had driven her to the phone. Asking her sisters to meet her at Harv's BBQ for lunch. They'd ordered and eaten—Lily picking at her food more than eating it—before Haley asked, "Are you going to tell us about it or not?"

At which point Lily shrugged. The whole triplet thing, knowing each other so well—she'd have thought there'd be none of that with the three of them. Other than their womb time, and the first ten months of their lives, they hadn't known each other until adulthood. She'd lived almost twice the number of years without them as she had with them.

And still, as Haley and Tabitha remained silent, just sitting there watching her, she admitted, "Asa and I slept together."

Both woman hissed in excited breaths.

"No, no," Lily told them. "He says it can't happen again. That it'll ruin our friendship."

She didn't tell them what Esme had told her about their growing up. About her fear that her brother would never let himself fall into romantic love or marry for real. But it had been on her mind a good part of the night as she'd lain awake in bed.

"The thing is," she said slowly, "I don't know how I'm going to survive when the marriage ends. I'm afraid my heart is going to be too crushed…"

"That's the most drama I've ever heard out of you," Haley said. The words might have been off, in the moment, if they hadn't been offered softly. With obvious compassion.

"You'll survive as you always have, Lil," Tabitha said then, with equal caring evident in her tone. "You're the strongest one of us. You're like a rock compared to me…"

"You survived the loss of the love of your life, while pregnant, giving birth to twins, and now are raising them all alone," she told her sister. "I'd hardly think living alone in an apartment and working at a café as giving me any real strength."

"How many foster homes were you in?"

"Eight." What did that have to do with anything?

"Eight times you entered a residence, looking for home. For family. Eight times you were forced out again. And here you are, loving with your whole heart. That's strength." Tabitha's eyes were steady and unwavering as she said the words.

"He clearly cares a great deal about you, Lil,"

Haley said then. "Maybe it won't progress any further than friendship for him. But maybe it will. Do you want to cut off the possibility before you have the chance to find out?"

She didn't. Of course she didn't. And she thought of something else, too. Haley finding her and Tabitha. She'd had no idea what she'd find. What kind of reception she might receive. Her sister had been facing possible rejection, anger, indifference. And still, when she'd turned eighteen and had found out that she had triplet sisters, she'd gone full force to find Lily and Tabitha. And then to write to them, asking them to meet.

Because that's what love did. It put itself out there, made itself available.

It didn't run and hide for fear of being hurt.

And neither did she. Just as Tabitha had said. She stayed in a home for as long as it would have her, hoping that she was becoming family.

The thought was firmly on Lily's mind as she pulled onto the ranch half an hour later on that Monday. She'd thought about refusing to have sex with Asa if the chance ever came up again. About stopping it if it started.

And knew she wasn't going to do that, either.

If love was going to have any chance to grow, she had to let it live freely.

And if it ended up killing parts of her spirit, irreparably damaging her heart, she'd find a way to live with that, too.

All of which didn't stop fear from striking her as

she parked in the house's garage, climbed into her four-wheeler and headed toward the office. What if Asa really did start to resent her? Like he feared would happen. To the point that he didn't want her to work on the ranch?

And what if a tornado hit them and wiped them all out? The thought sprang to mind.

Along with a well of sadness for what wasn't.

For her of all people, who'd never had a home like her sisters both had, to be the first of them to get married—and have it be fake...sometimes fate was a little cruel.

She texted Asa to let him know she was back and was just heading inside, when she got a text back asking her to come down to the petting zoo.

They'd talked about getting in a couple more animals. A llama, for one. With all of the families already booked for the summer, they were going to be bringing in enough money to hire a full-time caretaker for the zoo animals as well.

And once word got around about the rodeo activities, the dedicated wedding lodge, and other improvements and updates, they'd likely end up booking out completely months in advance. Asa knew his stuff. He had already put out feelers with his contacts who would send people his way.

And that was without the Fortune family in town spreading the word. Which was already happening.

They would need more staff. But for now, he must have had some day visitors descend on the petting zoo, for him to need her help.

Expecting to see several cars in the visitors' lot as she passed, Lily was surprised to see only two, belonging to the guys who'd come in early to go fishing. Kids were in school. Maybe a school bus had descended that she hadn't known about?

Things were relatively quiet, as a Monday in March would be.

Peaceful. Though she was looking forward to the craziness of summer in a way she never had before. To spend all day, every day with families vacationing on the ranch…she couldn't wait.

Pulling up to the petting zoo, Lily frowned. No one was there. The animals weren't even out. Just one of the horses.

Why did Asa need her help? Was one of the animals sick? Or more than one? They were all stalled separately, lambs with lambs, ponies with ponies, rabbits and ducks and…

She jumped off the four-wheeler and went inside the barn that housed the animals. And stopped when she saw Asa standing at the gate leading into the outdoor "zoo" area. Facing the barn door. As though he'd been waiting for her. Major stood beside him.

Oh, God. Please don't let anything be wrong with his horse. Major was Asa's immediate family. The one creature who had his whole heart.

"What's up?" she asked him, approaching slowly.

He didn't say anything for a long minute. "Asa?" She was almost up to him.

"Come on," he told her, grabbing her hand and

pulling her toward the opened gate. Major walked just behind them, right on his owner's heels.

The horse was more doglike in the way it served Asa. Followed him. Stuck by him.

Asa let her go as they stepped outside. The area had fresh straw on the ground, looking newly cleaned and ready for visitors. Only the one horse was there.

"What do you think?"

"About what?"

"Her." He nodded toward the horse.

That was it? He'd bought a new horse? She walked over to the obviously young mare. "I don't know all the much about horses, Asa," she told him. Lily knew how to ride—she'd been fostered on a small ranch when she was thirteen—but that was about the extent of her knowledge. "She looks gorgeous."

Going up to the horse, wanting to be of use to Asa if he was asking her opinion on something, she ran her palm along the mare's neck, not even sure of the breed.

She loved the softness. The warmth. And when the horse turned, putting her nose to Lily's neck, she held the mare's head to her. "She's lovely," she said then. "How old?"

"Two."

They'd have at least twenty years with her then…

"What's her name?"

Asa came up to stand beside her. "She doesn't have one yet."

So he was thinking about buying…

"She's yours, Lil. She's purebred quarter, from the best lineage in the state. I bought her this morning…"

Lily heard him. Noticed Major nosing the freshly laid straw a few feet away from them. As though he was keeping watch from afar.

She shook her head. "I don't get it."

"Family, Lil." Asa's soft words dropped into her world like little stars. "I've got Major. You've got her. She's all yours. For as long as she lives…"

Tears sprang to her eyes. She couldn't help it. Fighting hard to blink them away before he saw them, she pressed her cheek to the side of the young horse's head.

That he'd get the horse for her…and give it to her where she'd last been with her parents…

It meant the world to her.

"I love her," she said, hiding her face against the horse's shoulder, petting her. Not wanting to let her go. "Thank you." So much more wanted to tumble out. She gave it all to the horse instead. In long steady, warm caresses.

Asa was there, in the background, watching. "You want to take her out? She's saddle broken. Major can show her around the property…"

Hell yes, she wanted to.

She wanted to throw her arms around her husband, too. To hold on tight and tell him how very much she loved him.

Instead, she hugged the horse and said, "I'm going to name her Laura. After my mom." And didn't even care that her throat caught with emotion as she said the words.

Asa, in his own way, had just given her another part of her heart's desire.

Immediate family to call her own.

Family that wouldn't stay behind if she had to move on, but that would go with her, as Major always went with Asa.

Family that would be there when she needed her. That would need her, too.

Family that would be with her for however long their forevers lasted.

Asa knew.

He understood.

And he'd given her Laura.

Because the horse could give Lily what Asa could not.

He might not be able to be the husband she wanted, but he was the best friend a woman could ever hope to have.

Chapter Thirteen

Asa was still giving himself a thumbs-up for buying Lily the horse later that week, still feeling the high that had come over him as he saw how much the gift had meant to her.

Other than sex, he'd never seen her let go of the band of steel she kept around her emotions—until Laura.

It was a high he figured he didn't have to lose. Even after the divorce, he could still find little ways to give to her, to keep that smile on her face. Lord knew it wasn't a hard thing to do.

She'd had so little given to her growing up, the woman was grateful for a new toothbrush.

He'd found that out when he'd run into town for some things, had picked up a new toothbrush for himself, and had given her the second one that had come in the pack.

You'd have thought, by the smile on her face, the way she'd looked at him, that he'd bought her another diamond.

Maybe, if they were still married by her birthday, he'd buy her a pair of those, too. Diamond earrings to match her ring.

They'd added another meetup to their daily routine. Before dinner each night, they took Major and Laura out. Sometimes the ride was only fifteen minutes or so, but they did it together, looking out for their property he'd told her the first night he'd suggested it. And giving the horses some exercise.

Not that Major needed any extra. Asa was on the horse as much during the day as he could be. Riding Major in lieu of taking the four-wheeler, more and more often.

They'd taken to dropping Lily off at the house, to fix dinner, while he and Major led Laura back to the barn. By the time Asa had cooled and bedded down the horses, dinner was ready.

As he stood on the porch Thursday night before bed, sipping the rest of the beer he'd had as he'd gone over the books Lily had brought home for him to inspect, enjoying the stars in the vast night sky, Asa could hardly believe he'd reached such a perfect place in his life.

And when he heard the door open, and the small thump of Lily's boots stepping outside, he figured he'd finally found his own true Narnia.

A ranch of his own. A best friend who shared his business acumen and a love for the place. And a town with both of his sisters living in it. He and Major had finally hit gold.

"I'm firming up the guest list for Esme and Ryder's wedding next month," Lily said, "and I haven't heard back from your cousin, Bear. I sent his invitation to the address Esme gave me, somewhere across state from here. I'm figuring, maybe he doesn't know who I am. Have you heard anything from him?"

Asa shook his head. "I knew Bear as a kid, of course, but I haven't seen much of him since we grew up. I'm not even sure what he really does for a living."

"Esme didn't know, either. She just told me to check with you, in case you knew more."

He shrugged, thinking back to some of the few fun days he and his cousins had spent together as kids. Times when their parents hadn't been fighting with their spouses. Or off having affairs. "It's possible he wouldn't RSVP and still show up," Asa said then. "Keep a place for him, just in case. It'd be cool if he was there…"

More family back together.

Without the fighting.

Asa had never thought, before the previous year, that they'd all be living in the same town and growing closer by the week.

Bear would probably be as shocked, and maybe as pleased, as Asa was.

Finally finding a place where he wanted to stay.

A place to call home.

Lily leaned against the porch railing next to him. Reached for his beer bottle and took a sip.

Something she'd done before, at the bar, when she didn't want another one, but wasn't quite done partaking.

It had been his suggestion that she share his, the first time she'd expressed the predicament, a month or so after they'd met.

Tonight, seeing her full lips covering the nose of his bottle, he was instantly hard.

Something that had never happened in the bar. Not even close.

"What?" With her lips hanging open for the edge of the bottle, Lily stopped midsip to look at him.

Asa stiffened. He must have been staring at her. "Nothing," he told her.

Taking another sip and then handing him back the bottle, she said, "Tell me you'd rather not talk about it, or to mind my own business, but don't lie to me, Asa. Please."

She didn't look away.

On the contrary, she was standing right up to him. Not letting him off the hook.

Something else new.

And because he respected her—because he wanted to keep her friendship and receive the same courtesy in return—he said, "It really was nothing. Just when your lips touched the bottle…it reminded me…"

He let his words end there. No point in filling the moment with any more erotic imagery.

She licked her lips.

A natural response to having them talked about.

And it took every bit of strength in the whole of Asa's body not to lean over and kiss them. Instinctively, he knew she wouldn't stop him. It was in her body language. The way she was still there in the moment with him, holding her ground...

"I'm going into town," he said, overwhelmed by the tension, the wrongness of wanting something that would ultimately hurt them both.

And leaving his beer bottle sitting on the rail, he turned and strode through the house, out the side door, and didn't slow down until he was strapped into the driver's seat of his truck.

He didn't look back. Just drove. Needing lights. Even if it was just streetlights and those emanating from the Corral's front window.

He needed distraction.

Time to cool down. To breathe.

He could do this. Would be fine. They were just learning how to do it all—run the ranch while living together as friends who were pretending to be married. There were bound to be some stumbles along the way. They'd figure it all out.

He'd intended to just drive it off, but by the time he reached town, a full-blown fog had fallen. Asa pulled into the park.

What in the hell was the matter with him? He'd been hanging out with Lily for eight months or more, with no problem. Why was he suddenly having a problem keeping his hands, his lips, the rest of him to himself?

Was it the proximity?

Because, he had to face it, at the Corral, there hadn't been a chance in hell of kissing Lily without an audience, so it had never been an issue.

Was that really it? That he was really such a player that he had to have any woman he was alone with? Ones that he liked, of course, and who liked him back.

Ones who wanted it.

Yeah that must be it, he reassured himself. It was just a sexual thing...

His thoughts suddenly broke off as he was distracted by someone in a hoodie. From the slight build and average height...he couldn't tell if it was a man or a woman...or someone he knew...but he watched as the person went up to the community bulletin board. Attached a note to it.

He got out. Figured shooting the breeze with someone else, even a total stranger, would be better than sitting alone in his truck making an inconvenience into a way bigger problem than it needed to be. But before he'd taken his first step, the person had hurried away. Asa couldn't even tell in which direction because of the fog.

Still thankful for the distraction, and curious, he went over to the bulletin board anyway. The whole situation struck him as a bit weird. After all, who came out late on a foggy night to leave a note on a community bulletin board?

He didn't get his answer. But when he saw the note, he needed to know who'd left it more than ever.

The note wasn't signed.

And it wasn't just any note.

51 died in the mine. Where are the records?
What became of Gwenyth Wells?

What the hell?

He didn't know the gritty details, but he knew enough. His grandfather had been involved in that mining disaster that had happened long before Asa was born. And not in a good way. From what he'd heard, his grandfather, Edgar, had been at least partially to blame. And had run off…

Which was why Asa had only just been introduced to Chatelaine, where his Fortune ancestors had lived.

Grabbing his phone, he took a photo of the note and sent it in a group text to his great-uncle Wendell, his grandfather's older brother, and to Freya Fortune, the widow of his great-uncle Elias, asking if either of them knew who Gwenyth Wells was.

Freya had been the one who'd written letters, bringing Edgar and Elias's grandchildren, Asa and his cousins, to town the previous summer to receive their portion of the inheritance their great-uncle had left them.

It was late. Wendell and Freya were probably long in bed.

But they'd see the text first thing in the morning and be aware of what he'd found before anyone in town started talking…

As he was putting his phone away, Asa saw the open text message as he'd left it, except that there were little dots scrolling, as though someone was typing. Figuring it was Freya, who he knew sometimes had trouble sleeping, he stood there waiting for her response. Would she want him to remove the note?

Would that be ethical?

The dots were gone. And a new text binged.

Not from Freya.

It was from Wendell.

Yes, Gwenyth Wells was the widow of the foreman who died in the '65 mine disaster and got the blame for the collapse from Elias and Edgar. Her family was ruined. I don't know much beyond that.

Asa was heading back to his truck when his text binged again.

Freya had finally sent a response.

Oh, how awful, no wonder her name was familiar. Elias must have mentioned it over the years in sorrow.

Shaking his head at his family history, Asa climbed back in his truck and headed home.

Elias and Edgar Fortune had left a dead man's widow thinking her husband had caused the collapse, when they'd known full well it had been their own fault.

Somehow, feeling desire for a woman he couldn't have didn't seem like such a horrible cross to bear.

And unlike his uncles, he'd do the right thing.

One way or another, he'd figure out a way to quit wanting to have sex with his temporary wife.

Because, also unlike his uncles, he had no intention of losing friendships or leaving town.

Lily was devastated. Full-out falling apart inside. Pacing the dark, from kitchen to front porch, she wore an imaginary path in the wood floors Val Hensen had had redone before she'd put the place up for sale.

Asa had gone to town. Why? To be with another woman?

No, he wouldn't do that to her.

Or to himself. He wouldn't be *that* guy.

But he'd do just about anything to not have sex with Lily. And they almost had…again. After only making love with Asa a couple of times, she already recognized that look in his eye when he was losing himself to desire for her.

It was a heady look.

One she'd never seen before on a man's face. At least not directed at her.

If she'd turned away, Asa would still be there with her.

She should have turned away.

Easy to see from the outside looking in, but when they'd been standing out there…she'd been captivated by the powerful want between them, too.

No way she could have walked away.

So he had.

He'd told her where he was going.

To town.

Close to midnight on a Thursday night. She knew full well what there was and wasn't to do in town.

Meet up with someone.

Or go to the Corral.

There were no other choices.

Except, maybe, going to another town. Where he could take care of his needs without anyone in Chatelaine, anyone who knew Lily, finding out about it.

Stop it.

At the door out to the front porch, Lily paused. Staring out.

Could see writing on the wall almost as though it had been printed in big letters across the night sky. Her nights with Asa, being married to him, would be repeats of the current one. Him leaving at night, even to go into the Corral just to drink.

Something he used to do with her. Their precious time together.

Now his time to get away from her.

Turning, she started her trail back across the room again. She had to buck up. To lift her chin and look for the good. In just a couple of weeks' time, her entire life had changed. Giving her more than she'd ever thought she'd have. Making dreams come true that, in her previous twenty-nine years, she hadn't even come close to achieving.

At the kitchen sink, she glanced out, could see lights in the distance. She knew one of them was the security light at the barn where Laura was probably sound asleep.

Stomping her foot, as though she could crush that night's pain beneath it, Lily headed toward the stairs. When had she ever wasted time walking around feeling sorry for herself?

She needed to go to bed. Get some rest. She had a busy weekend, and an equally hectic week ahead. More check-ins, and a lot of renovating to oversee to get the ranch as ready as it could be for a full summer. And the following Saturday, just eight days away, was her and Asa's wedding party. In the back room at the Corral.

They'd agreed one night over dinner, the day that they'd both had texts from their sisters telling them to save the date, that they had a ton worth celebrating. The ranch. A home—albeit hers would be changing, it was still out there someplace, waiting for her to find it. But no matter where she ended up living, the two of them would be working here together long into the future. A forever friendship. Even Laura's advent into their lives was a true blessing. So, while others celebrated the legalities of a marriage certificate and rings on Lily's and Asa's fingers, the two of them would be toasting to having found the futures they'd dreamed of having.

In her bathroom, Lily scrubbed her face. Hard.

Getting rid of the grit that had tried to take over her mind downstairs.

Just standing in that bathroom, in a real home,

she had so much more than she'd ever had. And she wanted Asa in her life, as best friends—forever.

It was all well and good to reach for dreams.

But not to the point of killing a different version of a dream that had actually become reality.

Chapter Fourteen

Asa awoke on Friday feeling as though he'd managed to walk across fire and not get burned. He'd faced temptation with Lily and had gotten them both out of the situation before flames had consumed them.

And he knew that having done so once, he could do it again. As many times as necessary. He'd found the wherewithal to beat the demon that had been threatening their lifelong friendship. For however long desire continued to tempt him, he'd just get in his truck and drive. He had his escape hatch.

With the success giving buoyancy to his step and lifting his mood, he sought Lily out in the office midmorning. There were no more check-ins due until late that afternoon. And no checkouts. Everything else could wait.

"You feel like getting lunch in town?" he asked her. And then, so as to ward off any hint of a return of the demon, quickly added, "I have to make a stop and would like you to go with me. We could order takeout, make the stop, pick up lunch, and eat it on the way home."

Home. His and, for the next several months, hers.

The thought brought no threat. No feelings of danger.

Just…satisfaction.

"Of course," Lily said, standing. "Where's the stop?"

"My great-uncle Wendell's." It felt right, taking her with him. Not for show—though formally introducing Lily to the Fortune patriarch would further solidify their marriage in the eyes of anyone who could possibly have doubts—but because something truly weird was going on. Something worthy of mention to someone he trusted most.

And Lily was his someone.

His best friend.

She'd stopped at the edge of her desk and was looking at him. Frowning. "Why would we be stopping there?"

Only then did it occur to him that Lily wasn't just his best friend. She was also the woman who'd grown up in foster care and, until recently, had lived in a tiny old apartment, and had worked serving food to others in a café.

"You're going to love Fortune's Castle," he told her then, grabbing her purse, handing it to her and heading toward the door. She wasn't a foster that no one kept for long anymore.

Hadn't been for a long time.

She'd become a woman who would do anything for anyone. Who put others first and always found the good in any situation. Who brought a smile with her into pretty much every moment of her life.

And for the time being, she was his wife. As far as he was concerned, that meant she would always be a Fortune.

And before they divorced, he would see to it that she never, ever felt like she had to hesitate again before walking in anywhere.

Lily listened as Asa told her what he'd seen in the park the night before. She picked up on his escalated energy, his need to find out why on earth someone would have left a note about a decades-old mine collapse.

More, she felt almost light-headed with relief to know that he hadn't gone to the Corral to drink without her.

Or to seek comfort in a woman.

He'd driven to the park.

And parked.

The thought brought the threat of tears, and to avoid them, she tuned in to what he was saying about Freya Fortune. She already knew about the letters his great-aunt had sent to him and his siblings and cousins. Everyone in town did. But the fact that Freya had said that her late husband had probably mentioned knowing the mining foreman's widow after Asa texted her about the mysterious note he'd found tacked to the community bulletin board the previous night, *was* intriguing.

And... Asa was taking her to his family's famed castle. She could hardly believe that she was actually going to see inside the place known all over the state for its elaborate feat of architecture, hidden rooms, and supposedly secret messages buried in the cement. She'd heard that Wendell Fortune's art collection was impressive as well.

She'd driven by the place more times than she could count.

And now Asa wanted *her* to be a part of that piece of his family legacy.

Like he was giving her an official admittance into the Fortune family.

Shaking off the lofty thought, Lily spent the rest of the drive reminding herself that she was and always would be...herself.

And that self took things as they came. She didn't get dramatic and fanciful.

Those were the types of emotional forages that could take the cheer right out of a woman. Or a little girl being shuffled from home to home.

Still, she couldn't help the sharp intake of her breath at her first step into the renowned masterpiece. The place was huge, with high colorful ceilings. She could only imagine all of the hidden messages in the barrage of art, and as they walked through to the room where Wendell sat, waiting, she really found the place kind of bizarre.

Fascinating, ornate, and glamorous, but an odd thing for a man to build as his family home.

She'd seen Wendell before, of course, as Martin Smith, the man he'd been posing as all of her life. He'd been at town functions. A ribbon cutting in the park.

She'd glimpsed him often enough to know that the man in the big ornate chair, who welcomed them in with kindness, but not a tone of warmth, had truly grown frail.

"Thank you for seeing me," Asa said to the patriarch, his formality reminding her that he'd only met his great-grandfather's older brother the previous summer. "First, I wanted to introduce you to my wife, Lily."

The old man nodded. "I've seen her. One of the Perry triplets. Terrible tragedy there…" Wendell shook his head, and Lily warmed up to him in a way she'd never ever have expected to.

One of the town's founding fathers, or a relative of such, knew about her parents. Knew that she'd been born a triplet to loving people.

She and her sisters and parents had been *memorable*.

It didn't change anything about her, or her life.

And yet…in a strange way…it did.

If nothing else, it changed how she viewed herself.

"Secondly, I just keep thinking about last night's

note," Asa told his great-uncle. "Do you have any idea what became of Gwenyth Wells?"

Wendell's chin quivered a bit as he said, "I don't, but I remember that she was ruined. I heard that she knew that my younger brothers were responsible for the mine collapse." He lifted a shaking hand about an inch out of his blanketed lap, then let it drop. And continued, "She knew that they were the ones who'd placed the blame on her husband, the mine's foreman, who died in the collapse." He paused again, the wrinkles at his neck moving with the breaths he took.

Because Asa sat silently, so did Lily.

"It was rumored that she'd vowed to seek vengeance on Elias and Edgar, but they'd already fled town," Wendell continued after the brief pause.

Sitting on the big leather couch with Asa, Lily wanted to place a hand on his thigh as his grandfather was mentioned. She settled for leaning enough that her shoulder touched his.

"And she was never heard from again?" Asa prompted the older man. "Did she have any relatives in the area? Any other family?"

"She had a daughter, Renee, I think her name was." Wendell frowned. "She was a handsome young woman, as I recall. Seventeen or eighteen. Sure gave her father a sleepless night or two." Wendell's tone lightened, though the man's expression didn't change much.

"So is she still around? Married? Going by a different name?"

Wendell's headshake was minimal, but there. "She

left town with her mother soon after the disaster, and I never heard of either one of them again until last night."

"So what do you think of the note?"

The old man shrugged and readjusted the blanket across his knees. "My guess…someone's playing a prank. Or is out to cause a stink. These young kids today…just don't have enough hard work to keep their minds out of trouble."

While Lily didn't agree with that statement—she figured today's kids had way more to deal with than even she had growing up, with all of the information coming at them instantly all day long—but she understood Wendell's views came from an era when even kids worked on the ranch from sunup to sundown. With education coming in as a luxury. Or at the very least, coming in second.

And she told Asa as much a short time later as they stopped in town to pick up their lunch and head back to the ranch.

There followed a conversation about the internet and social media, and the pressures they brought—as well as the plethora of mind opening information—all the way back to the ranch. They didn't judge the past against the present. Didn't even compare. They just talked.

Sharing thoughts. Impressions. Memories.

Just like any of dozens of evenings they'd spent together at the Corral.

They didn't talk about his family's history. Or the

fact that Wendell Fortune knew who she was and re-membered her parents.

But there was comfort in knowing that she and Asa knew those things about each other.

Knew that they came with emotional investment.

And held the information safely.

Because that was what best friends did.

Asa woke every morning with a sense of antici-pation. Finding the life he'd dreamed of even better than he'd imagined. Far better.

It wasn't just hard work so that he could be the boss of his world. It was taking on all kind of tasks, challenges, being creative, and getting to meet inter-esting people among the vacationing strangers who were happy to share his property.

It was about knowing that Lily was sharing the days with him. That had been his missing piece. Not doing it alone.

Plus the fact that she was loving the work as much as he was—the challenge, the opportunities to grow something bigger and better—was a satisfaction he hadn't even known how to conjure up. And the knowledge that she wanted to continue to be his part-ner on the ranch even after their marriage ended? Well, that was more than he'd ever have envisioned for himself.

The days all rolled by one after another, each one different in the tasks that cropped up, and each one the same, too. There were no days off. Not until they'd gotten a firm grip on every aspect of the business, made some initial changes, and hired a few more staff.

But he and Lily had started taking a little more time, when they could, for their afternoon ride. It had become kind of like the Corral to him, those hours with Lily, he on Major and her on Laura, instead of on their barstools.

Up on separate horses, there was no danger of anything physical cropping up between them, just as there hadn't been sitting at the bar at the Corral.

And they could talk about whatever came up between them.

Like the upcoming wedding party being thrown for them. He was uneasy every time he thought about it. Such a public display of pretense. Everyone there together all at once. The ones who knew them best. He figured he and Lily needed a strategy—some kind of plan they could work out together—but wasn't sure what it would be. Or, even how she felt about the gathering.

Not that she'd share her feelings about it with him.

The one thing he and Lily rarely talked about— the one thing he couldn't ever remember hearing her talk about—was her personal emotions.

Not that he was any scholar on that front himself, it was just…with all of the women he'd ever dated—and there'd been enough to have a pretty good cross section—he hadn't had to wonder about what they were thinking or feeling. They'd all made it pretty clear.

Good and bad.

Like when he and Lily had run into Baylor Minser on Main Street. The woman had left no doubt of her disdain for Lily.

Or her willingness to take Asa on whatever grounds he offered. Married or not.

Lily hadn't shown any obvious reaction then, either.

On Thursday afternoon of the following week—with the party only two days away—he rode silently, trying to work out a way to approach the topic. They were out on a longer ride, checking all of the ranch's wooded hiking trails. Their current one was an easy, flat family trail that wove by a natural little rock waterfall into the small creek that ran through part of the property.

"Sometimes, when we're out here, I can't help wondering if it looked the same when my parents took our stroller on these paths," Lily said, throwing all party strategy conversation starters out of his mind. "It's almost like I can see us here with our whole lives stretched before us…"

The words stunned him. Or maybe it was her tone. Whenever she'd mentioned her parents in the past, it had always been with cheer. But her voice had changed before it had drifted off completely.

Filled with a longing so acute, he felt inept to deal with it.

Slowing Major to a stop, Asa glanced over to see the unusually melancholy look on her face. And pictured a ten-month-old baby version of her. He felt his heart swelling with sorrow for her. Regret. That little triplet girl had had parents, a father who'd have given her away at her wedding, a mother who'd have intervened with common sense when Lily announced she was marrying her best friend so he could get his ranch.

Or so he thought. Because in his gut, he knew it was wrong for her to go to a party filled with everyone she knew and cared about, pretending to be something she was not. The lie would be with her forever.

As would the divorce.

Even if the failed marriage was all his fault, she'd still be the woman who'd only been married six months. The one who'd made the poor choice to wed him.

Even if it was for the best reasons. To help a friend. And reach for her own hearts' desire in the process.

"They'd be proud of you, Lily," he said, feeling inane, and yet, confident, too, as the words came with a power that forced him to deliver them.

She shrugged, looked at him, and started to speak, but a call came over the radio with a crackle, followed by the voice of Jack, one of Asa's two full-time ranch hands. "A stray dog's been running through the cabin area," he said. "He's got no collar, looks like he's been on his own for a while, kind of mangy, too skinny. Mixed breed. About thirty pounds. Brown and white. I tried to catch him but he ran off. We're taking care of the barns and corrals now, making sure the entrances are closed and he doesn't get in and spook the animals…"

"We'll keep an eye out," Asa replied when Jack

had finished detailing the steps being taken, wishing the interruption had come at any other time. Lily hardly ever spoke of her parents. She'd been opening up to him—needing him?—and when she heard the message, set off immediately in search of the dog.

That was his wife, always putting others before herself, but at what cost?

Would there come a time when the pain the woman bore silently and alone rose up and damaged her happy spirit?

Was being married to him contributing to that cost?

Asa didn't like the questions.

Or their probable answers.

Chapter Fifteen

They'd be proud of you, Lily. As Lily listened to
Asa talking to his ranch hand, warning him about
the stray dog and making certain that the barns and
petting zoo were being checked, the entrances closed
off, she kept hearing Asa's earlier words ringing simultaneously in her head.

She sighed. More than anything, she hoped they
were true. Glancing around a 360-degree perimeter
of land in sight, she saw trees, with spring leaves just
starting to show up in force. And acres of ground
with the residue of crushed fall leaves, twigs, and
branches broken by storms. All was still. Quiet.

Peaceful.

No evidence of a dog running wildly through the
woods.

The horses would surely notice, as well, if another

animal was in their vicinity. Both of them were standing calmly, Laura's head just a foot from Major's
thigh. Major, probably bored by their slow pace—
and the fact they'd now stopped altogether—looked
about ready to take a nap.

And…the path ahead of them on the trail…it
jogged off to the left. Then immediately right. Then
left again. Like an S. And in the middle of the jog,
a red oak tree.

A curve around a tree…

Heart pounding, she slid down from Laura, keeping the horse's reins loosely in hand, to lead her ahead
of Major and Asa. Toward the small double curve.

It couldn't be, could it?

Her hands were shaking so hard as she pulled out
her phone that she had to push twice to access the
picture gallery. The photo she wanted was the first
one in the gallery.

The last one taken.

It was a photo of a photo.

One Val Hensen had found in some old ranch
boxes she'd been going through and dropped off to
Lily earlier in the day. Lily had snapped the phone
photo and put the original in the office safe. Needing
time to process it on her own before doing anything
else with it. Or telling anyone else about it.

Including telling her sisters.

Glancing from her phone, to the S the trail made
in the ground, and the placement of the tree in that
formation, she knew she had to be seeing things.

It couldn't be the same.

She was just emotionally in over her head. How could she not be? With her fake Vegas wedding, then the work at the ranch and planning Esme's legitimate marriage, and her and Asa's wedding party looming on Saturday…it was a lot to take in.

Lily wanted to believe that was all that was happening. Her mind playing tricks on her. And yet…

"What's up?" Asa had come up behind her.

She turned without thinking, paying no attention to the tears on her cheeks. She was that far gone.

He didn't ask again. Just took Laura's reins out of her limp hand, tied the mare and his gelding to a couple of trees and walked back over to her.

"It's too much, I know," he said, his tone softer than normal. Compassionate. A sound she'd heard directed toward his beloved Major before. "I've been trying to figure out a way to bring up the party on Saturday, and just…"

Shaking her head, she cut him off. He'd thought she was crying in front of him because of a party she'd get through, just as she'd come through every other difficult moment in her life? She'd planned to enjoy herself Saturday night.

Making the most of a gathering that starred her and Asa together.

Wiping her eyes, swallowing the emotion, she bucked up and handed him her phone.

"What the…" The way he glanced sharply from her phone to the trail had her heart thumping all over again.

Could she possibly be right?

She saw him look at the phone again. Enlarge the clearly old photo. Look at her.

And then… "Look at the tree root." Followed immediately by, "Is that… Oh my God, Lil. It's you and your sisters, in your stroller, with your mom, isn't it? Right here."

It couldn't be. It was just too…

She glanced at her phone again. But hadn't needed to. She'd stared at the photo so long that morning that it was forever ingrained in her memory. She was the middle one. Tabitha's hair was lighter. Haley's face more beautifully round than Lily's oblong features.

When the tears started down her face again, there was no way Lily could contain them.

She was standing on the very ground her mother had stood on, pushing her and Haley and Tabitha, and looking like the happiest, proudest, woman on earth.

He reached for her without thinking. Seeing Lily cry…tore him up. She wasn't a crier. *Ever.* And now…he had no idea what to do. How to console her.

There was nothing he could fix about the current situation. No way to make the past better for her.

Or less painful.

But when her arms slid around him, holding him, he could let her do that. Could embrace her, just as tightly, be there for her, a friend at her back—or wrapped around her—so that she knew she didn't have to be alone anymore.

He didn't try to find words. There were none.

Holding her firmly around the waist, pressing her body against his so that his presence, his warmth was solidly there—ready to support her completely if she started to fall—he stroked his other hand through her hair. Slowly. Again and again.

Not patting her head, either. Truly caressing her hair, across her head, over her shoulders, down her back. Even losing his fingers in its silky lengths, hoping that it felt good to her, could reach her, in the midst of whatever agony she was allowing herself to release.

Good with the bad, that's what she'd always told him. The way she'd always gotten through any hardship was to focus on the good.

He had to give her good to focus on.

When he felt the bone-deep shudder against him, he slid his hand under her hair, going straight for her back. With both hands. Running his fingers slowly down each side of her, still pressing her to him.

She'd never really been sobbing, just, in pure Lily fashion, quietly crying, but then her breathing changed, giving him the impression that her tears were abating.

Until it changed again.

To a rhythm his senses recognized.

And responded to. With his groin.

Her arms around his neck tightened, and she lifted her head from his chest, looking up at him.

She didn't say a word, just looked.

And he knew she'd felt the hardness that had sprung up against her.

But he wasn't pulling away. No way he could tear those soft, feminine arms from the warmth they were clinging to.

No way he'd add his rejection to her grief from a lifetime of loss.

She needed him. He was not going to let her down.

He'd be strong.

For both of them.

And he was.

Right until her lips lifted and planted against his. Her eyes had been wide-open as she'd done so.

Her gaze connected to his.

She'd moved slowly. Watching him.

And he'd watched her, too.

Knew the second she closed her eyes.

Just before he felt those soft, smaller lips touch his bigger ones.

There was nothing tentative about Lily's kiss. Nothing at all weak.

But the caress was most definitely filled with need—of a different kind.

Surging with sudden flame, he kissed her back, let her lead him down to the ground by the old oak tree, and then led her toward the dance that was coming.

It wasn't slow or sweet, but frantic and hungry.

She kicked off one boot while he pulled down her jeans and got both of her legs free. She went for his belt buckle. The fly was so tight he had to help with the button and the zipper, and the second he sprang free, he slid into her.

The ride was his shortest ever. A few strokes. She came. He came.

And there they were, half-naked on one of their family hiking trails, with their horses tethered just feet away.

He'd tried to give her a feel-good rub on her back. But the intensity pouring through her had obviously needed much, much more than that to counteract it.

She'd reached for the good.

And he was glad he'd been there.

Had been about to tell her so when Major snorted, Laura stepped back, and a flurry of fur came charging through the woods in the distance, aiming straight for the half-naked people lying on the ground.

Asa had his pants up and was sitting down, in front of Lily, before the dog almost reached them and then veered away. Still watching them.

"You can go after him," she hissed, as she scrambled to get back into her jeans, pull them up and then, sitting down, pull on her boot. She didn't kid herself that what they'd just done designated any change in their relationship or future plans.

Worst case, he'd had pity sex with her. But she didn't really think that, either. Asa was virile, and she was the only woman in his life for the next several months.

"Stay down," he said, not moving. "He ran from those running after him. Let him come to us."

Still reeling from everything that had happened,

half-numb, all emotion spent, she did as he asked. Boot on, she remained completely still, expecting the dog to get so close and then, change directions and head off.

Instead, as it approached again, it slowed, tail wagging, and came closer.

Head down, it stopped a few yards away.

Reaching into his pocket, Asa pulled out one of Major's sugar cubes and held it out to the dog. "It's okay, boy," he called softly.

Lily, who'd had a couple of dogs in her growing-up years, pets that had been with the families she'd entered and stayed with them after she was gone, held her breath.

Somehow, awash in so many different emotions as she was, it seemed as though, if the dog would come to them, that somehow meant that she and Asa were okay.

Dogs could sense trustworthiness.

He didn't run right up to them. Didn't approach at all at first. But his nose started moving the second Asa reached his hand further out. And with each sniff, he came closer. One step at a time.

Asa took out a second cube. Held it in his other hand, closer in, and slowly, with those cubes, eased the dog in until he stood there of his own accord.

She expected Asa to grab him then. Gently, of course, but to make sure the dog didn't run off again.

Instead, he petted the dog's head.

His back.

Reminding Lily of the way he'd first comforted her such a short time before.

She smiled. "You're a good boy, aren't you?" she asked the dog, in a tone of voice she'd use for a child.

She didn't reach out for him. She had no sugar. And didn't want to scare him off.

The dog looked from Asa to her, and then, to her complete shock, he came right up to her, sat on her lap, and gave her a lick on the chin.

Burying her face in his fur, choking back a new wave of tears she'd thought completely spent, she hugged him, kissing his mangy fur. And finally, when she was emotionally able, stood, still holding on to him.

She couldn't ride back with him. She wasn't that strong.

But she could carry him to the horses. Still holding him in her arms as she approached Laura, she turned to trade the dog for Laura's reins as Asa untied the horses. Laura didn't wait for Lily to get the reins. The young mare moved with Asa, straight toward Lily, nudging the side of Lily's head softly with her own.

Much like the dog had sat in her lap.

A complete stranger.

They knew.

It was like, on some level, Laura and the dog were telling her she wasn't alone.

Almost as though, for those moments, the animals had claimed her as theirs.

She'd never ever felt so loved. She really did have

her own family. A growing one. Laura, for sure, who was all hers. And Asa, her forever friend. Maybe her family wasn't a conventional one. It wasn't mom, dad, and the kids. But her dream was coming true.

She'd come full circle. Right there, on the same exact earth where she'd been Lily Perry, precious triplet baby whose mother glowed with happiness just because she and her sisters existed.

As she handed over the dog to Asa and climbed up on Laura for the trip back, Lily truly felt like her parents were there in her midst, smiling.

In her mind, they were happy to see her so loved.

And, in that moment, she was truly happy, too.

Chapter Sixteen

Asa needed space. Time to breathe in air that didn't contain an excess of…everything. The confusion of feelings that had bombarded his life would not get the best of him.

He just had to have a chance to rope them one by one and get them back where they belonged. Most of them in the ether, where they would evaporate and mess with him no more.

He'd called the animal shelter as soon as he and Lily had returned to the house with the dog. No one had called looking for their pet. While he'd given the dog a bath, figuring him for part cocker spaniel and maybe some small shepherd breed, Lily had made up fliers to post around town, inserting, as the last piece, the newly cleaned dog photo Asa took for her.

She'd insisted, without any fight from him, that

they'd make certain that the dog ended up in a good home.

While she made up a chicken and rice concoction to feed him, Asa gladly escaped to head into town to put up the fliers, and to stop at the GreatStore for dog food, treats, and maybe a toy or two.

Before he pulled out of his drive, he texted the picture he'd taken of the dog to Devin Street. Asa had only met the man a couple of times, at the Corral, but he'd liked him. Respected him. Owner of the *Chatelaine Daily News*, Devin not only got wind of everything going on in town, he was also known to foster dogs.

He was barely on the road before his phone rang.

"You got a new dog, man?" Devin asked as he picked up the phone.

"He was running loose on my land. You recognize him?"

"No. He's a cutie, though."

"You want to take him?"

"I would, but I'm fostering a huge Great Dane at the moment, and believe me, you wouldn't want a little one around here right now. Chumley's all I can manage..."

Sharing an understanding chuckle with the man, Asa told him about the flyers he'd be putting up and Devin said he'd keep his ear to the ground.

Asa's first stop was at the community bulletin board. The note he'd seen put up the other night was still there. Seeming to glare at him with unanswered questions.

He tacked his dog flyer on the opposite end of the board.

And spent the next forty-five minutes on Main Street, going from place to place to ask permission to hang his lost dog missives.

The task itself wasn't such a time suck—it was all the chatting, backslaps, and well-wishes he got every place along the way—congratulating him on his wedding.

Asking him how married life was treating him.

All reminders of the very things he'd needed to escape.

He'd left his sister's place on Main Street for last—wanting to get a look at the progress she was making. And also to see if there were problems, if she needed help, if anyone was giving her a hard time in the final stages of creating her down-home Western-style restaurant.

In other words, his usual MO.

Cowgirl Café was slated to open the following month and if there were any snags, he'd be there to help her through them. Bea had always loved to cook. But that didn't mean she was on top of every aspect of opening her own business.

"Wow, this is impressive," he heard himself saying once inside, giving her a hug as he looked around. The post and beam interior and Western flavor looked far better than he'd envisioned them when she'd first told him about the place.

"You want to see the menu?" she asked, pushing one beneath his nose. "They just came today."

Taking it, he read the list of solid cowboy/cowgirl favorites, from five kinds of chili and corn breads and poboys to mac and cheese in crocks.

"Now you've made me hungry," he grumbled, handing it back to her. "I don't suppose you have any samples back there." He pointed to the opening that led to the kitchen.

"Go home to your wife, little brother. She just called to say she over made the rice and is doing up a chicken and rice casserole for dinner. She wanted my mushroom sauce recipe…"

There'd been a bounce in Bea's step from the second he'd walked in the door and caught sight of her. The smile that was on her face as she sassed him went far beyond her mouth, too. Her eyes seemed to glow in a way he hadn't seen in a long time.

"Yes, ma'am," he retorted, as she took one of his fliers from him before he'd even offered it to her.

"She told me about the dog, too, now git. Knowing you, you still have to stop at the store and the casserole will be coming out of the oven in less than an hour…"

"You know, bossy bosses aren't all that popular…" he told Bea with a grin as he grabbed her for a quick kiss to her head, and left.

Feeling better than he had since he'd pulled his pants back on after being with Lily in the woods.

His sister hadn't looked so excited about anything since her divorce, and her happiness made him happy.

Turned out, buying dog stuff wasn't such a bad gig, either.

Figuring it was best to overbuy rather than end up not having something Lily wanted, Asa bought up two grocery bags worth of food, treats, and toys, and grabbed a dog bed, too, on his way out of the aisle. The stuff could all go with the dog when he went home.

Or be donated to the shelter if the dog's owner didn't want them.

He had a feeling the supplies would make Lily happy.

And that lifted his mood, too.

The dog—Max, she was thinking of him in her mind—occupied Lily before dinner, through it, and afterward, too.

Turned out, he was a chewer.

And a clinger. He didn't like to be alone in a room for long.

He was also house-trained, she discovered just as the buzzer was going off, indicating it was time for her to get Bea's casserole recipe out of the oven, and Max went to the door and whined.

She didn't have a leash or collar yet, so she grabbed the rope Asa had fashioned to serve as both holster and lead when they'd first found him. Slipping it on Max, she took him out. He did his business so fast it was like he'd held it to the last minute.

And she made a note to self to offer him outdoor opportunities more often.

She wasn't calling him by any name. Wasn't letting herself start to think of him as her own. But having been a foster, she wanted to be a good foster parent, even if only for the night.

The dog's presence made Asa's return much easier to take in stride. Not only did the little guy wiggle and wag and demand attention, but he was like a third in the room. Allowing them to avoid talk of what had happened between them in the woods.

"I think he's still young," Asa said as they finished up dishes together, and he asked her if she wanted to have a beer on the porch. "The chewing, and the overexuberance seem to point that way."

He had a lot more experience with dogs. Was probably right.

"I choose to think that he's just thrilled to not be running scared in the woods." After all, fosters had to stick together.

"That, too." Asa chuckled, tipping his bottle to her as they each took one of the two big white wooden chairs, with a holstered dog lying down between them.

As though he'd accepted that he had a place for the night and exhaustion had finally hit him.

"This is nice," Asa said after a few minutes of relaxing night air filled only with the sounds of an occasional breeze. The birds that chirped and called their various melodies during the day had settled in for the night as well.

And all Lily could think about was the sex she and Asa had had earlier.

It had been different. Not just sex between a hungry man and woman, but between her and Asa. Best friends with an understanding of the other's needs, insecurities, and motivations.

Where she got that notion, she didn't know. She acknowledged to herself that he might not have experienced anything of the sort. But the way he'd reacted to that photo of her mom and sisters and her... it was as though he'd been right inside her heart. He'd felt her.

She'd felt him in there. Sharing her anguish.

Right before they'd ripped one another's clothes off.

"This is paradise," Asa murmured. "This right here...it's what I longed for as a kid but never had."

"You don't remember a time at all when your parents got along?"

He sipped from his beer, staring out into the night, and shook his head. "Nope. I think my dad's affairs started early in the marriage. Mom's came later."

"And you guys knew about them?"

"It was kind of hard not to. They threw them in each other's faces. And then threw my aunt's and uncle's liasons in each other's faces, too, as though that justified their behaviors." He shook his head.

And she hurt for him.

She thought of what Esme had told her about Asa's lack of belief in a true love that lasted. His sister thought Lily had cured him.

If only that were possible...

"I love that you called Bea for recipe suggestions tonight," he said then, sliding a glance her way.

Lily smiled. "It's nice, having a group of people with various skills who are happy to hear from you and help out."

"It's called *family*, Lil," he said, laconically, but kindly, too. As though he was pleased.

The word got her. *Family.*

His sisters would only be her family for a short time and then...

She'd stood on the exact spot where her mother had stood with a heart full of love for her.

She still couldn't wrap her mind around that one. To the point that, other than Asa, no one else knew. She'd thought she'd call her sisters, but with the dog, and well...everything, she hadn't done so.

Silence fell between them, and he sat forward. Turned to her. "You and I, we're family now," he told her. "You married me. Took my name. And even after the divorce, we'll be family. We promised each other forever."

Her throat clogged to the point that she couldn't speak. She wouldn't let tears fall. Not in front of him again. Not in the same day.

So she nodded. Sipped from her beer.

He knew that having grown up without a family to call her own, family meant everything to her. Being a part of one was her heart's biggest desire. The only dream she cared to reach for.

She thought about the two of them. Her past... and his. How it affected them both. Envisoned the future, what it would probably look like. What it could look like.

What she most *needed* it to look like.

And when she could speak calmly, normally, she found herself saying, "The Hensens were married almost fifty years, worked together every day, and the way Val talks about her husband, their love holds true ever after death," she said. And then she talked about one of her high school teachers who'd opened her home to Lily for a graduation celebration because Lily had been living alone in her one room apartment by the time that June had come around. The woman Had been near retirement. Had been married for over forty years. Had grown children of their own. And they'd worked together to give Lily a special day of her own.

"I didn't know they'd done that," Asa remarked, glancing her way. "That's such a cool thing. Why didn't you ever mention it before?"

For the same reason she hadn't told anyone except him about the picture she'd received that morning. The things that meant the most to her were cherished inside where they couldn't get crushed.

Just as the things that hurt the most weren't talked about, either. She wouldn't shine a light on them. It would only give them the power to hurt more.

"It just never came up," she answered. "The point is, Asa, there are happy marriages. A lot of them. You must at least hope that Esme and Ryder will be happy together for the rest of their lives…"

She wasn't sure if he shook his head, or just gestured with it. He'd stopped midmovement to take a long swig of beer. "Of course, I hope it," he told her. "But I don't feel certain that will be the case. When you watch relationships erode, one day at a time, you see what happens... I don't know how some do it. I just know that I can't take that chance."

He glanced at her, and though they were sitting with only the light from the front window, she could see the steely resolve in his gaze. "How could I gamble like that? On the possibility that we might come out okay? Because if we're wrong, I lose you."

She smiled as best she could. Nodded. Then looked out into the night.

"I can't lose you, Lil."

At the sincere emotion in his tone, she glanced over at him. Smiled for real, and said, "I can't lose you, either, Asa."

And told herself, as they took the dog and went upstairs that night—and Asa veered off to his own room without any hesitation at all, asking her if she wanted to keep the dog, or have Asa take him—that she had to give up on the idea that she and Asa would ever have a real marriage.

Or children to share it with them.

He cared about her deeply.

Loved her even. As a best friend.

And that was far better than anything she'd ever had.

It was just that she'd just begun believing in the possibility that she could have whatever her heart desired. Or that she could at least keep trying for it, keep reaching, until the day she died.

As long as she kept believing.

With that picture of her own mother looking so gloriously happy with her babies firmly in mind, alongside Asa's support and lovemaking that afternoon, she felt like she was at a crossroads.

And wasn't sure which path to take.

Chapter Seventeen

Lily was already down in the kitchen, feeding the dog, when Asa came downstairs after his shower the next morning. They'd agreed not to call their new companion by a name since they didn't know what his actual name was.

They'd both already figured the dog had had an owner, even as young as he was, because he'd been neutered.

Listening to Lily talk to the four-legged bit of happy energy as he headed toward the kitchen, he hated to think about her giving the dog away again.

But when it happened, he knew she'd take it all in stride. With a smile on her face.

Lily was used to losing what she cared about.

Which was why he had to get his ass in better gear

for her. Keep his hands off her. Get divorced, and settle in for the forever part of their vows.

He couldn't let himself think about happy marriages.

He would *not* be one of her losses.

"I had an idea for the ranch last night," she told him as he came into the kitchen to prepare his usual bowl of cereal and toast, while she munched on her granola bar and a banana.

The words, the easy tone in her voice, settled some of the tension inside him. He knew he hadn't given her the answer she'd wanted the night before. And had been half prepared to deal with a new distance between them.

Instead, so Lily-like, she was forging into her future at the ranch.

Breathing a silent sigh of relief, he said, "What's that?"

"I'm thinking maybe we look into a horse therapy program…"

She paused just as his toast popped. Reaching around her to grab it from the toaster, he met her gaze.

And smiled. "I think it's a great idea," he informed her, moving quickly away. "The ranch I was on before I moved here had a program, and while I was skeptical at first, it was really kind of cool. They worked mostly with displaced teenagers. Horses have a natural ability to sense human emotions and even just the nonverbal support was a thing to see…"

"I read about a place once, when I was having to

leave another home. It was a boarding school that offered equine therapy outside of Corpus Christi, and I wanted to go, but..." She tilted her head back and forth. "Clearly I didn't have the money."

"Did you ever mention the idea to anyone? Or try to find out more?"

He wasn't surprised when she shook head. "What was the point? My monthly foster care amount wasn't nearly enough. It wasn't like I knew anyone with money, and I saw no point in getting my hopes up, or wasting anyone else's time, when I knew it wasn't going to happen."

Because she didn't reach for what she wanted.

Or she hadn't. Until she married him.

And now she was thinking about other teens like herself, wanting to provide for them.

If it was possible, Asa's pool of love for his best friend grew even deeper.

Leaving the dog, with his new holster collar and lead, at the barn with Asa later that morning, Lily went into town to meet her sisters for lunch.

She'd thought she'd tell them about the picture Val Hensen had given her, but wasn't quite ready to share yet. For so long, her sisters had had family, while she hadn't.

For a minute or two, she wanted to savor seeing who she'd been, all on her own.

Tabitha had the adoptive mother she'd grown up with. Haley, the mother who'd fostered her, and was her mother still.

Their mother was all Lily had. She wasn't ready to share. Her sisters would get their copies of the photo. It was theirs as much as hers.

She wasn't trying to be selfish, or in any way slight them. But the photo was just such a huge thing for Lily, representing so many things. She needed some private time to process.

They'd have questions…suppositions…especially Haley, whose journalist brain couldn't stop digging. And Lily wasn't ready to start wondering yet.

She'd grown up knowing her parents had been killed in a car accident. But had never wanted to know more. Because doing so would make it bigger, more painful, within her.

Yet seeing her mother's smiling face…she kind of did want to know…as though, her mother deserved for Lily and the others to find out, to have her daughters know her as completely as they possibly could.

But not that day. Lily was already riding on crests too high to sustain her, over undertows strong enough to take her down.

Which was why, as soon as Asa had left the house that morning, she'd called Tabitha and Haley to request a get-together. They were the only ones who knew the truth about her marriage.

She'd told them both she'd needed to speak with them before her wedding celebration the next night.

Who she was, what her marriage was, where she was going…she couldn't seem to get straight in her own mind and heart about it. She'd spent much of the night lying in bed with her heart and head fighting each other. Another first for her.

In the past her heart had just shut up.

She'd eventually invited the dog up on the mattress with her, and, with his warmth pressing her through the covers, had finally fallen asleep.

Only to wake with the same battle raging inside of her.

There was no rush to figure it all out. She was under no time constraint except her own emotional one. She needed to have something right within her before she went to that party with Asa.

As soon as she'd opened her eyes that morning, she'd known she had to talk to her sisters. Haley was practical—she'd take the mind part of the war. And Tabitha…was a mother. She'd be the heart.

Maybe, listening to the two of them go back and forth with their opinions, she'd see where she needed to be. Who she sided with most.

By previous agreement, the three of them connected in the diner's parking lot, but before Lily could even get more than a thank-you out, a woman she'd never seen before came up to the three of them.

"Do you know if there's a hotel in town?" she asked, leaving Lily to wonder how the young woman could have missed it. It wasn't like Chatelaine was all that big.

"There's just one motel," she answered, figuring the unknown woman, with her wavy short brown hair and green eyes, had just broken up with someone, or found out some other bad news. She seemed distracted—and not in a happy way. "It's called the Chatelaine Motel," she continued. "You can't miss it, it's right at the tail end of Main Street here. It's an old two-story motor lodge with rooms that open onto the parking lot, has a second level walkway and is desperately in need of some updating. But it's clean."

She was babbling, wanting to help, needing desperately to unload on her sisters, and getting odd vibes from the stranger in their midst.

"I'm Lily...Fortune," she said then, stumbling over the last name in her attempt at friendliness, at which time Tabitha rescued her with, "I'm Tabitha Buckingham and this is our sister, Haley Perry."

"We're known around here as the Perry triplets," Haley told the younger-looking woman.

So weird, as soon as they tried to be welcoming, the woman kind of turned away from them, hunching her shoulders, as she half mumbled, "My name's Morgana," and hurried off down the street.

Haley, always the journalist, watched her go. "Interesting," she said, with that needing to know more tone in her voice. "She definitely didn't want to give her last name. I'll bet there's a story there."

"Yeah, she did react kind of odd..." Tabitha was saying, as Lily moved them toward their destination.

Lily had no focus for Haley's penchant to make a story out of everything. She'd only squeezed out enough time for a quick sandwich before she had to get back to the ranch. With it being Friday, they had two check-ins that afternoon. And then it would be tomorrow and her and Asa's celebration would loom...

If nothing else, she needed to let her sisters know she might need a little help keeping up appearances at their soiree. They deserved to understand why, after all the trouble they and Esme and Bea had gone to throw the party.

As it turned out, she only ordered coffee—because it's all her sisters wanted and she was glad for the faster service. And to not have to choke down food.

"I need to talk to you both about Asa," she said as soon as they had their cups in front of them, Lily on one side of the table, Tabitha and Haley on the other.

It just felt better to her that way.

"What's up?" Tabitha asked the question, but both sets of eyes were trained on her, sending compassion in waves.

Which was exactly why she'd called them. She wasn't all that good yet at sharing private details of her life with her siblings, but for some reason, it suddenly all came tumbling out of her. Probably more than should have. *Way* more than Asa would have wanted to share. She told them more about making love on the couch in Vegas on their wedding night. About the night on the couch at the ranch. And then, leaving out the part about the photo and the S in the trail, about having had sex with her husband in name only out in the woods the day before.

She didn't mention the dog, either.

"He loves you," Tabitha said softly, a smile on her face.

And Lily shook her head, saying, "He loves me like a friend. He's not *in* love with me. Every time, as soon as it's done, he reverts back to just friends. We've had sex, but we've never slept together. Or even been in bed together. And when I tried to talk to him about giving the marriage a real chance, he adamantly refused."

Haley swore mostly beneath her breath.

"Did he say why?" Tabitha asked.

Lily gave her sisters the abridged version of the things Esme had told her, and then added, "In his mind, to try is to risk failure, and he'd rather have me as a forever friend than take a chance at losing me."

Tabitha's eyes grew a little moist. Haley raised her brows and shrugged.

"So you just have to show him differently," she said, shocking Lily. Haley was supposed to have been on her *give-up-on-him* side of the battle. The side who knew she wanted children, and if he wouldn't give them to her, she couldn't settle for less.

"I agree," Tabitha told her. "You're head over heels in love with this man. How can you even consider giving up on a chance that he'll change his mind?"

Lily's heart clunked at that. She'd been so deafened by her own inner war, she'd failed to think about Tabitha's having lost the love of her life to death.

Failed to even think about the fact that her sister knew exactly when it was that you had no chances left.

"People change all the time." Haley's tone was unusually soft. She started pointing then, as she threw out a list of to-dos. "Play the femme fatale," she suggested. "Make him see you as more than just his buddy. Be the woman in his life. Do your nails. Put on makeup. Buy a sexy teddy. Hit him where it hurts."

Lily glanced at Tabitha, who was nodding. Could something that...doable...really work? It wasn't her, but neither was dressing up as she had for her wedding. She'd done it once, so she supposed she could pull it off again. All except Haley's last suggestion. She had no desire to ever hurt Asa. Period.

"And I'd talk to him some more about it, too," Tabitha said. "Let him know that as long as the two of you keep open communication, and work at it, you can get through the tough times."

Something Tabitha hadn't had a chance to do with her baby's daddy.

But it made sense.

Reaching over, Haley slid her opened hand beneath Lily's on the table and then clasped her fingers. "Bottom line, though, sweetie? You have to trust your heart. It will tell you when to go, if it comes time to do so. Until then, you keep trying."

That. Right there. Truth rang loudly within her. Settling both her heart and her head.

Giving Haley's hand a squeeze back, she reached for Tabitha's, too. "I love you both. You know that, right?"

It wasn't something she generally said aloud.

And she held her sisters answering avowals of love close to her heart as she insisted on being the one to pay for their coffee and headed for the door.

On the way to the rest of her life.

One way or another.

Lily was in the four-wheeler, escorting a family back to their cabin, when Asa got the call about the dog. The exuberant guy had been with Lily since she'd returned from town, and Asa headed up to the office, letting himself in with his key, helping himself to a soda from the cooler in the little store that took up one side of the reception area, and then heading behind the desk to drop money in the drawer.

He was killing time.

Waiting for Lily to return.

Needing to prove to her that they could make their future work. There at the ranch together. With their horses and other animals. Maybe even with them both living on the premises.

They'd have the best part of a lifetime partnership without the traps that eventually got to one or both parties and turned love into hate.

The dog came bounding in before her, dragging his leash, and he could hear Lily laughing at the boy's antics. The little guy ran in and jumped up on Asa, as though it was his job to welcome Asa to his own property.

Lily didn't look as happy to see him. "What's up?"

From her reaction, Asa could tell she knew he wouldn't be at the office at four in the afternoon if there wasn't a situation.

"I got a call about the dog." He started in and stopped when she interrupted him.

"I figured," she told him, sounding calm, businesslike. "As soon as I saw your four-wheeler outside. How soon is he leaving?"

"That's what I needed to talk to you about," he said then, moving closer to her. "It turns out that someone recognized him from the photo. There was a rancher renting a place just this side of town who moved on without warning, leaving in the middle of the night. The dog was his. And, it appears, was left behind on purpose."

Lily was staring at him. And he could read in her expression the things she wasn't saying.

"So...you want him?"

Eyes narrowed, she studied him. "Do you?"

"Yeah."

"Me, too." There was nothing businesslike or sedate about her as she ran around the desk she'd put between them and went straight for the dog, bending down to put her arms around him. "Oh, and, if it's okay with you, his name's Max," she informed him, before letting loose with a slew of baby talk that cut him out completely as she let Max know that he was home, and would be loved and have a happy life.

Max, Juniper, Sunshine...any name was fine with him.

As long as it brought that radiant smile to his wife's face.

"I think he approves." Lily looked over at him and giggled as the dog gave a lick across her chin.

Asa joined the two of them on the floor then, needing to be a part of the moment. To play with the dog—Max—and let him know that he was a part of them now.

He watched in amusement as Lily grabbed a toy and started playing tug-of-war with their new pup.

Max grabbed hold, pulled, and was growling playfully. Chuckling, Lily looked over at Asa, handing him her end of the rope.

Inviting him into their game.

Taking the rope, he pulled, but not too hard. He didn't want to break the young dog's teeth. Or get too rough with him, either.

When Max tired, helping himself to a drink from the dish Lily must have put down earlier, and then lay down, watching them, Lily sat there on the floor and smiled at Asa.

"Thank you," she told him.

"Right back at you," he murmured back.

And just like that, they'd become parents.

Chapter Eighteen

If Lily had had any doubts about the seduction she'd planned for Friday night—having stopped at the GreatStore on the way home to pick up everything she'd need—Asa's involvement with Max had silenced them.

As good as he was with a stray dog...she knew he'd be a hundred times better with a little human. The man was father material all the way. She'd had enough of them in and out of her life to be able to tell the greats from the maybe nots.

He'd grown up with a definite no for a father.

But that didn't mean that all men were that way. Asa being a case in point.

He'd done so much for her, and now she was the one who was going to have to fight for their future.

To that end, she had the night all planned out.

She took Max out and then, taking him with her, excused herself to bed while Asa was still going over bids and figures for some of the remodeling projects they'd talked about doing before summer. She needed their newest family member shut in her room, hopefully asleep on her bed, when she made her move.

She'd washed her hair that morning and covered it so it didn't get wet during her quick shower. The lingerie thing...she'd never in her life thought of herself wearing one.

It was one piece, red with black trim and lace, and mostly see-through. The silk garment came with spaghetti straps up top and snaps for an easy open crotch.

She felt naughty just putting it on.

Her first glimpse of herself in her bathroom mirror almost had her calling off the whole thing. And then she heard her husband's boots on the stairs and knew that she couldn't give up. She couldn't let fear—hers or his—win.

Shivering, noticing how clearly her tightened nipples showed through the fabric, she grabbed the makeup she'd purchased for her wedding day. Applied it as best she could as the artist had done it for her in Vegas. And then took her new, wide barrel curling iron and did her best to reproduce the waves the hotel's expensive stylist had created out of her usually boring, straight dark strands.

She'd looked at shoes, too, but the GreatStore's selection was most definitely not femme fatale, so she had decided to paint her toes and just go barefoot.

She'd done that, giving them time to dry, before pulling her socks and boots back on in time for check-in.

The one thing she hadn't done, in Vegas, or that afternoon, was go the artificial nail route. Her fingers lived on working hands, and that was just fine with her. She could dress up to please her husband at night after work, but she couldn't be dealing with pieces of plastic sticking out on the ends her fingers, worrying about breakage, all day while she worked. She'd smoothed and buffed her short nails, though. Lily wanted to tempt Asa, to show him a different side of her, not pretend to be someone she was not.

She was attempting to give him a lifetime.

Not a moment in time.

Asa had been upstairs fifteen minutes, long enough for his nightly rinse off—something she knew about because, for the past weeks, she'd heard his shower running as she lay in bed, picturing him naked in there.

Her time had come.

Unless she was going to put it off…give herself more time to think about it…give him more time to come around on his own.

Standing at her bedroom door, with Max snoozing on her bed, just as she'd hoped, she stared at the doorknob.

Was she chickening out?

Or being wise?

Hanging from the doorknob was the new shirt she'd purchased to wear to their wedding party the next night. Feminine. Silky. White. Would look great with the new black jeans she'd bought.

And…if there was any chance that a celebration of her and Asa's love could be for real…it was now or never.

She opened the door. Shivered as the cool night air hit her skin. Then turned the knob, held it, and let it slowly release as she closed Max in behind her.

Lily stepped lightly down the hall. Not to be sexy, but because she didn't want Asa to hear her until she was right there. In his face.

A seduction in the hall didn't have any ring to it.

Pulse racing, she faced his closed bedroom door.

There she was. Doing it. Just as her heart had directed.

A light shone beneath the door.

Was he reading?

Still in his attached bathroom?

If she just walked in with no warning, would she be interrupting something that was none of her business?

Maybe she should wait until the light went out.

Or…knock first.

With a shaking hand, she rapped lightly, once, and then reached for his door handle and turned it. Stiffened her shoulders. Feeling more like she was going into battle, not moving toward sex.

He'd been in bed—slept in the raw, she saw— but was halfway out of it by the time she stood in the doorway. His pillow was propped up, his tablet on the bed.

And...

"Lily? What in the hell are you doing?"

Not at all the response she'd expected. Perhaps she should have waited until his light was out...

"I'm hoping I'm about to have sex." The words tumbled out, sounding less awkward than she felt. "You're good at it, Asa. And while you aren't doing it with anyone else, and since we've done it before..."

In some part of her mind she knew that rambling wasn't sexy.

Nor were the words spitting out of her.

But the way he was looking at her...with some kind of fascinated horror...

She should have opted for the putting-it-off choice minutes before in her room. Given herself more time to think it all through.

Because he wasn't moving, or speaking, she took a couple of steps toward him, worried that she wasn't pulling off the teddy look after all.

Then stopped herself, just barely, from wrapping her arms around her chest.

When he didn't stop her advance, she continued forward, stopping only when she reached him, standing there nude beside his bed.

That's when she looked down.

And saw his body's response to her presence.

She was most definitely, gloriously wanted.

The sight, the knowledge it brought, emboldened her, and she reached for his chest with both hands, sliding her fingers through the springy hair there. Purposely gliding over his nipples.

Asa groaned. He reached for her.

And…

Gently pushed her away.

"We can't, Lil." His voice sounded strained. But then he moved briskly toward the pair of pants thrown over the chair in the corner of his room.

He had them on, up, and fastened before he turned, grabbed a robe off the back of his bathroom door, and tossed it to her.

"Here, put this on."

She did so at once. Not for his sake, but for her own. Never in her life had she ever wanted to cover up so badly.

But she wasn't running.

She'd been right to know she was walking into battle.

And, humiliation aside, her reason for being there was stronger than ever.

"We can't do this," he said, standing there in the middle of the room, his arms crossed.

"Yeah, we can. We've already proven that." Her words weren't planned. They were coming from a desperate place, a hurting place, that had been given free rein.

He shook his head, seemingly not the least bit affected by her continued presence in his room. "And as great as those moments were, Lil, we have to live platonically so that nothing gets in the way of our partnership, running the ranch, and most importantly… us. Our friendship."

"I know that's your take on it," she said then. "But

there are two of us here, Asa, and a true partnership has to consider both sides." She'd come up with that on the drive home that afternoon.

"Yes, when the agreement is being made," he countered, without even a pause to think about her side. "But our marriage, our relationship…that's a done deal. Based on a mutual agreement. One party can't just suddenly decide to change everything up after the deal has been signed."

The deal under which they'd signed their wedding license.

He wasn't budging. Clearly he had no intention on hearing her out.

Dashing her hopes.

Except…he wasn't throwing her out. Even as he rejected her, kindness emanated from him.

Because he cared that much.

It was that—the love he'd professed, the love she felt—that kept her from apologizing, excusing herself, and slinking quietly away.

Because their lifetime of living and loving together, of having a family, was at stake.

She might not get what she wanted.

But she could no longer live with herself if she didn't reach for her stars.

She wasn't leaving.

He had logic, fairness, decency, even rationality on his side. Everything that ruled successful interpersonal relationships.

And was in the right on a critical point that would protect them for the rest of their lives.

If it had been anyone else but Lily standing there, he'd have extricated himself from the situation.

However, he couldn't do that with her. Not just because they were legally married…but because he truly loved the person she was. He wanted her in his life. Valued her friendship more than any other single thing. All of which he'd already told her.

She moved and relief flooded him, until he saw that she was heading for his bathroom door, not the one leading her back to the hallway, to her own room, outside of his suite, which he could lock as soon as she exited.

His robe fell off her shoulders as she moved, and by the time he realized what she was doing, returning his robe to the hook on the back of the door, he was already hard again.

Staring at that incredibly beautiful body in the tantalizing piece of man-killing lingerie.

He wanted her so badly it scared him. Truly sent shivers of fear through him. How was he going to control his desire for her if she was throwing herself at him like that?

Knowing she wanted him made it a hundred times harder.

"You do realize that if we continue to have sex, I'm going to start wanting you like all the rest of the casual women in my life, right?" The words spewed forth out of desperation.

She stood her ground silently.

"Sex always brings issues—heightened emotions… expectations…and when one can't meet them, there are over-the-top disappointments, too…"

"We've already had sex, Asa. You can't undo that."

He didn't know how to get through to her. Almost panic driven, he gritted out, "You're asking for something I can't give you, Lil. Believe me, I want to give you everything your heart desires, but I can't do this." He knew his words were hurtful and regretted having to say them.

However, the stricken look he'd expected to see on her face wasn't there.

Instead, her gaze seemed to be filled with compassion.

"You're free to choose to give us a try, Asa, in a legitimate marriage. It's not that you can't. Esme was talking to me about the way you guys grew up. She told me about reaching too soon for love with her first husband, because she was so desperate to find what she knew was out there…" She paused. "It's clear that the acrimonious home your parents raised you three in affected you all deeply. And *differently*. I'm not saying there aren't valid reasons for your concerns. I understand where you're coming from. But it seems criminal to allow your parents' and aunt's and uncle's mistakes, and your fear of repeating them, to deny you your greatest happiness."

"I already have my greatest happiness. Right here." He raised his arm, encircling the air around him. "This ranch. And your friendship. The rest, the sex…that's transitory. It makes people do things, promise things, that aren't right for them, because in the moment, they're so consumed by physical need they can't think straight."

"Have you ever, once, promised anyone anything during sex?"

His tension grew. "No." Because he'd specifically made it a point to say what had to be said before he ever got to that point with a woman. Including her.

And yet...somehow, there he was.

"You have no guarantee that it will turn bad between us, Asa. We can talk things out...just like we are doing right now. We care about the same things—the ranch, the people in our lives. We honor family. I'm so in love with you that I can't fathom life without you. And you've shown me over and over that you care enough about me to keep my feelings in the mix, too. We wouldn't be having this conversation otherwise."

He heard all her words. But the *I'm so in love with you* part was what kept reverberating through him.

She couldn't be. And if she was, then it was up to him to save them.

"There've been a lot of couples who've made it work for a lifetime, Asa. We might very well be one of them. All I'm asking is that you give us the chance to have it all. A real family. Maybe even kids someday."

Kids. Like Esme's little guys. A flash of himself at the fishing pond, with little four-year-old Jimmy putting his hand trustingly in Asa's hit him. Along with his thought of having a son of his own someday.

But not at the risk of making an eventual enemy out of Lily.

"Kids are one of the top reasons married couples fight." Money and sex were the other two. He'd looked it up. "Because of the strong emotions they bring." Just like the other two. She was making his point for him and didn't even seem to grasp that.

"People fight, Asa. There's a difference between healthy disagreements, and the kind of acrimonious dissension you grew up with."

When he opened his mouth, she held up a hand and said, "Look, how about we just try it for the six months we agreed to stay married. I'll know, going in, that it's only a trial. If it doesn't work, we'll divorce as planned and be friends only…"

"But you knew going in that the marriage was going to be platonic and in name only." And there she was less than a month later, trying to change the whole agreement on him.

"But we both broke that original agreement, mutually, on our wedding night. And then again downstairs on the couch. And yesterday…out in the woods…"

His mind immediately shot to—and away from— that memory. It was one he knew he couldn't dwell on.

"I'm not trying to make you someone you aren't, Asa. If, after trying this, you still feel as strongly about not taking a chance on a real marriage, then I will respect that choice and still love you with all my heart. As forever friends. All I'm asking is for you to open your mind to the possibility of something *more*, and give us a shot."

For a second there, he thought about it. Seriously wanted to consider the idea.

But, though she had good talking points, he told his truth. "It's not just about the sex, Lily. It's about being free to walk away." He didn't know how to articulate what raged inside him, but he did his best. "That's what always brings you back, knowing that when you need a breather, you have the ability to walk away. In a marriage, you can't do that. In a marriage, you're promising *not* to walk away. And that puts chains around you. Chains made of expectations. And when the chains get too tight, you go into fight mode. It's a natural reaction. Instinct." Which was something no amount of talking, or even wanting, could change.

He knew the second she gave up. Her face flattened. Became one he recognized from his first months of knowing her. The face she gave to the world.

Hiding herself behind it.

And a part of him was relieved to have that friend back.

The rest of him just ached.

Chapter Nineteen

Lily hadn't planned a worst-case scenario.

She'd expected stipulations and conditions. But not Asa's point blank refusal to even attempt to see if they could make a real marriage work.

And his response to her mention of having kids with him?

That children were one of the top three reasons couples fought?

His definition of fighting between married couples, and hers, were vastly different. She'd lived in enough homes to get the gist of the whole husband and wife dynamic. Yes, there were definitely arguments. Strong disagreements, even, like when Sandy and Tom, her twelfth-year parents, had had to give her up to move to Wisconsin where he'd had a tremendous job offer. One that would allow them to afford lessons and opportunities for their own kids, including sending them to college. She hadn't been meant to overhear that particular argument, but it was one she'd never forgotten.

And what she'd learned was that when people truly loved each other, were honestly and wholeheartedly committed to each other, that love showed them each other when push came to shove. And, seeing each other, instead of just themselves, helped them to find what was best for both. And for their family.

Lily stood there, in her ridiculously revealing piece of cheap lingerie, and felt the cold, hard truth settle over her.

The problem between her and Asa was that they were not both wholeheartedly devoted to each other. She was fully committed to loving him forever. Had accepted that he was a piece of her heart and soul.

But to him, no matter how good things might be between them in bed, she was and always would be his freckled friend in the GreatStore uniform.

In his own way, whether he realized it or not, that was the truth he'd been trying to tell her all along.

She didn't blame him. She couldn't. After all, he could no more help how he felt than she could.

And he'd tried so hard to spare her. Had given her every piece of her heart's desire that he had to give.

But it wasn't enough.

And *that* was her truth.

She'd seen that look on her mother's face. The pure joy involved in pushing her babies in a stroller.

She might not ever have that, but she could no longer go through life without giving it her all. Her parents would expect that of her.

And she, an offspring of them, owed it to them, to honor the too shortness of their lives, by making the most of every moment of her own.

Lifting her chin, she looked the love of her life straight in the eye and said, "I can't do it, Asa. I can't stay in the house, sleeping down the hall from you, sharing groceries and furniture with you, knowing that there's no chance of us ever being a real family together." Instead of losing air due to a tight chest as she spoke, she found herself breathing more freely. Her voice growing stronger as self-honesty poured out of her. "I'll honor our agreement. I'll attend the party tomorrow night and pretend. I'll stay married to you for six months, and even live on the ranch, in the cabin you used to occupy. But that's it. I'm going to sign the ranch over to you this week. And when the six months is done, so am I. Here. And, maybe, with you."

She faltered there. Felt her throat thicken, but said, "If I can be happy meeting you at the Corral for drinks now and then, okay. But if not..." She shook her head and then settled her gaze straight on his again. "I want a real marriage, Asa. I want children. A home. I deserve a family of my own. And I don't think I'll ever find that as long as my heart is close to you."

Turning her nearly naked fanny on him, she held

her head high, her shoulders straight, and walked out of his room.

In her heart, she'd just walked out of his life.

Asa held his ground as Lily walked out. Told himself that she'd calm down. Change her mind. He went to bed. Even slept some. On and off.

In between bouts of waking up, having reality and panic hit him simultaneously, it took a great deal of effort to fall back to sleep.

Fortunately, by the time he was out of the shower Saturday morning, he was feeling better. On top of the fear and confident that everything would work itself out.

It always did.

Then he saw Lily's note.

She'd be taking care of the office for him in the short go, but he needed to be looking for a full-time employee to assume the duties as soon as possible.

He told himself it was just the disappointment and hurt feelings talking, that when a little time passed, she'd still want to work at the farm—not because of him, but because of her own attachment to the place. Because it was as much her dream to own the dude ranch as it was his.

And then he saw the Horse For Sale sign tacked up to the community bulletin board outside the public restrooms and showers by the pool in the cabin neighborhood.

Laura?

She was selling Laura?

Staring at the picture of the horse he'd bought for Lily, the horse he knew for certain she loved, he could no longer talk sense into emotions that were roiling through him.

She was removing Asa, and things associated with him, from her life in an effort to take back ownership of her heart and move on to a future that held her dreams.

To find her heart's greatest desire.

A family of her own.

Tearing down the sign—he'd buy the horse if he had to—Asa raced his four-wheeler back up to the office area, looking for Lily. Her four-wheeler was parked in its usual spot. As was her car.

He breathed a sigh of relief until he strode into the office, intending to drop the wadded up For Sale sign on her desk, to meet her calm, clear gaze, and hear, "Sorry for the note."

Finally. She'd calmed down. Was coming around.

Shoving the wadded-up paper into his back pocket, uncaring that there was hardly space for it, he accepted her apology with an, "That's okay."

"I just wasn't sure I'd see you this morning, and I want to give you all the time you need to find a replacement for me."

What?

Getting up from her desk, she let him know that ranch business was all in line for the day. Their part-time desk help was already on-site. And finished with, "I'm going upstairs now to pack my things. I'll be moving into the cabin before we head to the party tonight. What time do you want to meet up to head in?"

"Head in?" His head was spinning.

"We'll need to drive together tonight," she said, sounding like a waitress serving a customer. "To keep up appearances."

Right. Their wedding celebration.

"Six," he told her robotically. Not even sure what time they were supposed to be there.

"Okay. I'll meet you right here," she said then, and moving by him, leaving a good two yards between them, she walked out on him.

Again.

Asa turned to go after her. Took a couple of fast steps…to do what? *Say* what?

Frustrated, unable to find anything that sounded good to him, he kept walking fast. Just not after Lily. He got into his truck and drove into town. Not bothering with things like speed limits and turn signals.

Partially because there was no one else around who could be hurt by his actions.

But as soon as he hit city limits, he wanted to turn around and go back.

To what?

Instead he went to the park. The place he'd gone the night after he'd walked out after sex. Not only was it too early in the day for beer but things like alcohol and mouthing off didn't work when it came to his feelings for Lily.

He'd never had a friend like her. One who'd be

missed so much when he moved on that he'd think twice about going.

He walked around, mostly kicking rocks, feeling more pent up than ever, and headed back to his truck.

"Asa!" Spinning, he saw his great-aunt Freya heading toward him from across the street.

And thought about how lucky he was. Living his dream because of the older woman's generosity.

He greeted her with a smile. Asked how she was doing. Then walked with her toward his truck.

"You coming to the party tonight?" he murmured.

"I wouldn't miss it." Her words sounded strong. Certain. But she was frowning at him. "Except that, why do I get the feeling you're not looking forward to it as much as I am?"

It was almost as though she knew...

Guilt gnawed at him. Freya had opened her heart to him and his siblings and cousins, had moved to town to be near them, to watch them enjoy their inheritances, and he'd cheated to use her money to buy his ranch.

"I screwed up, that's why," he told her. Somehow thinking that if he owned up to the original wrongdoing, it would somehow be able to right the mess he'd made of his friendship with Lily.

Freya didn't seem fazed. "I've lived a long time and have seen a lot of wrong turns in my life. Usually turns out there are ways to right them." They'd slowed to a stop on the sidewalk in front of his truck.

"Not this one." He was working up the words to

tell her the truth, and when he opened his mouth to say them what came out was, "I lost Lily."

"You *what*?" the woman's near screech didn't sound at all kind or supportive.

"The way I grew up… I can't do a repeat. I told her so, thinking she understood, but she didn't. I love her, Aunt Freya. I told her that, I just…" And there it came. The news about the fake marriage, fashioned to get Val Hensen to sell him the farm. He and Lily writing their own wedding vows, pledging to be friends forever. Her telling him she was in love with him.

And confessed his own response, too. Almost word for word.

What a pitiful picture he made. Big tough cowboy that he was, in his jeans and tough boots, big shoulders casting shadows on the older, more frail woman in front of him—whining to her like a little kid.

The silence between them, when he finally stopped was a relief. He waited for her castigation. And probably her demands that he tell Val Hensen what he did and give her the right to void the sale of the Chatelaine Dude Ranch. For the Fortune good name if nothing else.

He was almost ready to hear it, too, when she opened her mouth. "It's very clear to me that you love Lily."

Not at all what he'd been expecting, and so the truth popped out. "Of course, I do. She's my best friend."

Freya's headshake made him frown.

"No, not just as a friend. As a woman. A wife. As a life and love partner."

Those last four words…struck him. A punch to the gut.

"Go get your woman, Asa. Make it right. Before tonight so you all can enjoy your wedding celebration for real."

Life and love partner. Exactly. Life and love best friend.

Life and love partner.

That's what Lily had been trying to tell him. They were already there. Living it. Except that he'd been too obstinate to see it.

Marriage. Husband. Wife. They were words. It was the people, their actions, and how they felt, that made them successful ventures, who gave their hearts and souls to the roles they'd vowed to honor for life.

And the chains…partners gave each other the freedom to express their needs. They listened with a need to understand. Not to change the other.

Just as he and Lily had done from the beginning.

Life and Love Partner.

Oh, God. What had he done? He had to get to her…

Bending, he gave the older woman a hug, and then, with barely a thank-you, jumped in his truck, backed up and sped out of town.

Before she could think about packing, Lily had to wash her sheets and pillowcases. She'd soaked the latter with tears during the night.

And again that morning.

She had to be done crying. And figured, the clean sheets would signify the tears' final demise.

Lily had no idea what she was going to do with herself once the marriage ended. But at least she'd have some financial resources. She was going to hold Asa to his monetary agreement with her, just as he was holding her to the friendship only part of their deal.

The thought of leaving town had occurred to her. She could go to college somewhere. Get far away from Asa, at least long enough to get him out of her system.

But Chatelaine was her home. The town was her family.

And no way could she lose her sisters again, after finally having them in her life. Tabitha was going to need help with her little guys as they started walking and getting into things. And Haley...she needed someone to remind her that life was more than unanswered questions. At least if she wanted to find love for herself.

Maybe Lily had been too hasty, quitting her job at the ranch. She loved the work.

And what better way to get over a man than to have him for a boss? To work for him every day and be around enough to see the women coming in and out of his life.

Maybe she'd even end up falling for whoever he hired as a new ranch hand.

When that thought brought more tears right as

Lily was folding her newly cleaned sheets, she sniffled and kept folding.

Then, leaving packing for another time, she took Max with her down to the barn and went to find Laura.

The dog needed something besides tears and a maudlin woman for company. She'd hugged him plenty, but had barely spoken to him since she'd returned to her room the night before. There was just no way she could find words for the chaos going on inside of her.

With Laura it was different. The mare was a female. And didn't need words.

She was also named after the woman Lily needed so desperately in the horrible aftermath of her botched bedroom encounter with Asa. Maybe if she'd had a woman who'd been through the ups and downs of adult romantic relationships, guiding her through every phase of her journey into womanhood, she'd have made different choices the night before.

Wouldn't have pushed Asa so far into a corner that he'd had to fight his way out.

Up on the horse, she rode for a while, feeling somewhat better as she breathed the fresh air, enjoyed the blue skies and sunshine. She didn't purposely head for the family trail with the notable jog around an old oak tree, but felt a little less alone when she saw it ahead of her.

And when she stopped at the curve, sitting atop her horse close enough to the tree to touch it, she knew it was right that she'd come to her mother as she, once again, saw her life heading into another rebirth.

She knew how to do it—how to re-create her home life. How to forge a place for herself wherever she ended up. And thankfully, she now had the money to choose that home for herself.

Of course, it would have to be a small place. She wasn't ever going to be rich. And maybe she'd have to take out a mortgage to finish it. If she built new.

But...

Laura's head lifted, turned back toward the trail they'd come down, snorted.

And then Lily heard it, too.

Horse hooves. Heading their way.

Putting a hostess smile on her face, expecting to see Jack, one of their ranch hands, with a guest rider, she felt her whole being slide into nothingness as Asa and Major appeared instead. Two strong male beauties. The one brought her a sense of comraderie. Acceptance. Understanding.

And the other...the muscled cowboy on top of the horse...looking so ruggedly handsome...ripped her heart a little more.

"Jack told me he saw you head this way," he said, as though he had every right to seek her out in her private time.

She nodded. Didn't want to fight with him.

Ever.

She loved him. Flaws and all.

Understood him.

She just couldn't be *in love* with him anymore.

When he rode Major right up to her, within a foot, she sat straight. Didn't flinch. Or give in to the temptation to give her mare's sides a slight nudge and gallop off with her into the sunshine.

He climbed down from the saddle. Then with a gentle tap of his hand to Major's front paw said, "Back."

Lily watched, starting to wonder if the man had been drinking.

She saw Major bow—one front leg bent under him as he went down—and hold the position. Lily was so busy watching the horse, it took her a second to realize that Asa had done the same. And was staring up at her.

"Lily Perry Fortune, will you please give me a chance to take that chance with you that you offered last night, minus the six-month getaway clause?"

Her heart pounding, she stared down at him.

"Asa? What are you doing?"

"I'm begging," he said, as though it was obvious. "I love you, Lily. Like a man loves a woman. You saw it. I think I did, too. I just couldn't get past my own deeply ingrained barriers to acknowledge what was right in front of me."

Tears sprang to her eyes again. She didn't bother to blink them away. After the night before, she hardly felt they mattered. "This is because I'm quitting, right?" she asked. "You want me to stay here on the ranch with you."

"I do want that, yes. But that's not why…"

Was he going to shatter her heart completely before he let her go? "Don't do this, Asa, please?"

"I have to, Lily. I love you."

He'd said the words to her before. They didn't change anything.

Major stood up. Asa did not.

"I want you in my home, in my bed, and to have my children."

She could hardly breathe through the tightness in her chest. Was shaking in her saddle. "Don't, Asa. It's not what you really want. Not what you believe in. Which means it will probably end up just like you fear it will."

He shook his head. "You're wrong."

She wanted so badly to believe him, she almost slid down off her horse to throw herself in his arms. But she couldn't fool herself anymore.

She'd never find her dreams that way.

"What changed between last night and today?" she asked him, finding the strength to resist him.

"Four words," he said, and for a second there, she went back to thinking he'd been drinking. Though, even that was so out of character it was hard to believe. Asa didn't drink during the day unless there was some kind of party, and he never drank to the point of talking out of his head.

"Four words?" she prompted when she could.

"Life. And. Love. Partner." He said each word like it was its own sentence. And then, "That's when I got it. Marriage, husband, wife…those words, what they stand for in my mind, scare the hell out of me.

But I am so in love with you, Lily, that the thought of losing you is making me want to sell the farm. Will you please be my life and love partner until death do us part, and beyond that, too?"

"Life and love partner," she repeated, her heart tumbling over itself in fear. On a race to a joy she couldn't let herself grasp.

"Aunt Freya... I told her what I'd done, that I'd lost you and she said those words. They clicked, Lil. They honest to God clicked. Because they described us exactly. It's what you said. We're partners who always consider each other's needs as well as our own. A person is only trapped if he can't get out, and as along as he is out, being heard..." He stopped, shook his head, as though he was getting too much to fast. "Please, please, will you be my life and love partner?"

With tears streaming down her face, Lily slid down off her horse, and would have fallen if her husband hadn't stood and caught her up in his arms, lifting her feet up off the ground with the exuberance and strength of his hug.

"I love you, Asa Fortune, and I'll very happily and sincerely be your life and love partner until death do us part and beyond," she promised against his neck, right by his ear.

He kissed her then, slowly lowering her feet to the path.

And as she kissed him back, she knew her feet were never going to touch the earth in quite the same way ever again.

Her step would be lighter because she wasn't walking alone.

No matter what the future brought them, she and Asa would live it together, until death and beyond.

Just like her mother's love had continued to live in Lily, even when Lily had refused to think about her.

Because love carried that much power.

The party was in full swing. With Lily in a sexy white blouse and black jeans, and him in his own white shirt and black jeans, they had walked in holding hands, to a roar of cheers and flying confetti. They'd made their rounds, taken ribbing and heartfelt congratulations, had fed each other cake, danced their wedding dance alone in front of everyone, and toasted champagne.

The pile of gifts was overwhelming and wonderful—mostly because of the look of awe on Lily's face when she'd seen them—and were being sent to the ranch for opening later.

She'd asked him for a few minutes alone with her sisters, and while Asa visited with everyone around him, he missed her. Had hardly been able to leave her side all day—not because anyone or anything was holding him there. Except his own desire to be close to his beautiful bride.

The need would dissipate to a more normal level of togetherness. He knew that.

Or, as Lily put it, faith in their togetherness would make it less necessary for them to be with each other every minute of the day.

He wasn't really buying it, though. It made sense to him that some life and love partners were just made to do life together—work and play.

As Lily had pointed out, the Hensens had done so.

And now he and Lily were carrying on their legacy.

When Val Hensen came up to him, giving him a warm hug, he hugged her back and said, "Thank you." He'd been thinking the words yet hadn't meant to say them out loud.

"You bought the ranch fair and square," she told him.

He shook his head, "No, thank you for forcing me to propose to and marry the love of my life," he told her.

And glanced up to see Lily, just approaching from the side of him. She'd heard his words. He could tell by the glow in her eyes.

She licked her lips. Just as she'd done out on the trail that afternoon, asking for a repeat of two afternoons before. And then again, after they'd moved her things into his bedroom. She licked her lips and he was lost.

"You trying to kill me here?" He leaned over to whisper in her ear, and then kissed her.

Longer and deeper than he probably should have in front of an entire town's worth of their family and friends.

The catcalls that rang out that time were mostly calls for the two of them to get out of there, and when he looked at Lily, and she nodded, he scooped her up into his arms and headed for the door.

They were almost outside when Tabitha and Haley appeared in front of them.

"You're a very lucky man," Tabitha told him, her eyes brimming with tears as she looked from him to her triplet in his arms.

"And a smart one, too," Haley added.

That was it, along with a glance that passed between the three sisters, speaking without words, messages he didn't need to know.

Messages that comforted him just the same.

Lily might have grown up without family of her own, but she'd spend the rest of her life swimming in it.

His. Hers. And theirs.

And, if he had any say in it, they'd start adding to it, too, as soon as nature gave them the chance.

He'd found his life and love partner.

And the dream he hadn't known to dream had found him.

* * * * *

Don't miss Bea Fortune's story,
Expecting a Fortune
by Nina Crespo

Available April 2024!

#3039 TAKING THE LONG WAY HOME
Bravo Family Ties • by Christine Rimmer

After one perfect night with younger rancher Jason Bravo, widowed librarian Piper Wallace is pregnant with his child. Co-parenting is a given. But Jason will do anything—even accompany her on a road trip to meet her newly discovered biological father—to prove he's playing for keeps!

#3040 SNOWED IN WITH A STRANGER
Match Made in Haven • by Brenda Harlen

Party planner Finley Gilmore loves an adventure, but being snowbound with Professor Lachlan Kellett takes *tempted by a handsome stranger* to a whole new level! Their chemistry could melt a glacier. But when Lachlan's past resurfaces, will Finlay be the one iced out?

#3041 A FATHER'S REDEMPTION
The Tuttle Sisters of Coho Cove • by Sabrina York

Working with developer Ben Sherrod should have turned Celeste Tuttle's dream project into a nightmare. Except the single father is witty and brilliant and so much more attractive than she remembered from high school. Could her childhood nemesis be Prince Charming in disguise?

#3042 MATZAH BALL BLUES
Holidays, Heart and Chutzpah • by Jennifer Wilck

Entertainment attorney Jared Leiman will do anything to be the guardian his orphaned niece needs. Even reunite with Caroline Weiss, his high school ex, to organize his hometown's Passover ball with the Jewish Community Center. Sparks fly...but he'll need a little matzah magic to win her over.

Get 3 FREE REWARDS!

We'll send you 2 FREE Books plus a FREE Mystery Gift.

FREE
Value Over
$20

Both the **Harlequin® Special Edition** and **Harlequin® Heartwarming™** series feature compelling novels filled with stories of love and strength where the bonds of friendship, family and community unite.

YES! Please send me 2 FREE novels from the Harlequin Special Edition or Harlequin Heartwarming series and my FREE Gift (gift is worth about $10 retail). After receiving them, if I don't wish to receive any more books, I can return the shipping statement marked "cancel." If I don't cancel, I will receive 6 brand-new Harlequin Special Edition books every month and be billed just $5.49 each in the U.S. or $6.24 each in Canada, a savings of at least 12% off the cover price, or 4 brand-new Harlequin Heartwarming Larger-Print books every month and be billed just $6.24 each in the U.S. or $6.74 each in Canada, a savings of at least 19% off the cover price. It's quite a bargain! Shipping and handling is just 50¢ per book in the U.S. and $1.25 per book in Canada.* I understand that accepting the 2 free books and gift places me under no obligation to buy anything. I can always return a shipment and cancel at any time by calling the number below. The free books and gift are mine to keep no matter what I decide.

Choose one: ☐ **Harlequin Special Edition** (235/335 BPA GRMK) ☐ **Harlequin Heartwarming Larger-Print** (161/361 BPA GRMK) ☐ **Or Try Both!** (235/335 & 161/361 BPA GRPZ)

Name (please print)

Address   Apt. #

City   State/Province   Zip/Postal Code

Email: Please check this box ☐ if you would like to receive newsletters and promotional emails from Harlequin Enterprises ULC and its affiliates. You can unsubscribe anytime.

Mail to the **Harlequin Reader Service:**

IN U.S.A.: P.O. Box 1341, Buffalo, NY 14240-8531
IN CANADA: P.O. Box 603, Fort Erie, Ontario L2A 5X3

Want to try 2 free books from another series! Call 1-800-873-8635 or visit www.ReaderService.com.

---

*Terms and prices subject to change without notice. Prices do not include sales taxes, which will be charged (if applicable) based on your state or country of residence. Canadian residents will be charged applicable taxes. Offer not valid in Quebec. This offer is limited to one order per household. Books received may not be as shown. Not valid for current subscribers to the Harlequin Special Edition or Harlequin Heartwarming series. All orders subject to approval. Credit or debit balances in a customer's account(s) may be offset by any other outstanding balance owed by or to the customer. Please allow 4 to 6 weeks for delivery. Offer available while quantities last.

Your Privacy—Your information is being collected by Harlequin Enterprises ULC, operating as Harlequin Reader Service. For a complete summary of the information we collect, how we use this information and to whom it is disclosed, please visit our privacy notice located at corporate.harlequin.com/privacy-notice. From time to time we may also exchange your personal information with reputable third parties. If you wish to opt out of this sharing of your personal information, please visit readerservice.com/consumerschoice or call 1-800-873-8635. **Notice to California Residents**—Under California law, you have specific rights to control and access your data. For more information on these rights and how to exercise them, visit corporate.harlequin.com/california-privacy.

HSEHW23